THE SWORD AND THE SORCERESS

CHRISTOPHER WOODS

The Sword and the Sorceress

Copyright © 2024 by Christopher Woods

CHAPTER ONE

Boggan's Tavern was filled with smoke and noise. I sat with my back to the wall at the furthest table from the door. It didn't pay to have your back to the crowd, it's a good way to get a knife in the ribs. I didn't have to worry about that too much at Boggan's but it was a good habit to cultivate. Half of the crowd in the tavern were off-duty Marines, many of us still wearing the tabard.

I sipped my ale as I watched a couple of Marines pushing one another. Fists would follow. No one would interfere unless blades were unsheathed.

A dark skinned server I had never seen before made her way through the crowd with a tray and several drinks. She dropped them off a few tables from me and dodged groping hands. Stepping away from their table she approached mine.

"You're a long way from home," I commented in Fallanasi.

"As are you," she replied. Her gaze stopped on the twin swords leaning against the wall beside me. Her eyes widened. "My Lord."

"No need for that," I said. "Just a Marine."

"A Sword."

"I haven't been a Sword for a long time. Just a Rhymen Marine, now."

"Does Rhyme even know what they have?"

I shrugged. "It's probably for the better. Life is so much easier without expectations."

She appeared to be lost in thought for a moment.

"Where did you go?"

"Expectations," she answered. "Perhaps we are in Rhyme for much the same reason."

"Could be."

She grinned and asked in Common. "Can I get you another drink?"

"Absolutely."

"I'd like one as well," a voice from behind her said. "Preferably wine."

The Fallanasi woman turned and drew in a sharp breath as she saw the woman behind her. "Yes, lady."

"Serafine," I said and motioned toward the seat in front of me. "Have a seat."

I understood the sharp breath. Sorcery in Fallanasi was typically an evil endeavor. It was hard to hide a person's skill in sorcery when it alters them physically. Snow white hair was a dead giveaway of a sorcerer or sorceress. There were other tells that could be picked up at a glance about what kind of sorcerer sorceress you were facing. Everything was right there in the eyes. Each type of sorcery brought out a color in the eyes of a sorcerer.

Most sorcerers could wield a single type of sorcery whether it be fire, water, earth, air, or even rarer, light and dark. A few could wield two sorcerous elements.

"Kort, how did I know I would find you here?" She asked as she sat down and stared at me with eyes filled with every color.

"Perhaps repetition."

She shook her head. "I'm not sure what draws you to places like this. Not sure I will ever understand you."

I shrugged. "Not sure why you even want to."

"You're my partner."

"I guess that's reason enough," I said.

"We have a new assignment," she said. "Sable district."

"Sable? That sucks."

"Yes. I really wish you hadn't pissed off Major Talent."

"In my defense, she never said she was his daughter."

"You're lucky he didn't challenge you to a duel. He's well known as a swordsman."

The Fallanasi woman almost dropped her tray as she snorted.

"Something amuses you?"

The server placed the wine in front of Serafine. "It's not my place to say."

"No, please explain."

"It would be the shortest duel in history, lady."

"Do you know Major Talent?"

"I do not need to, lady." She nodded toward me and continued. "He is a Sword."

She placed the ale in front of me with a small bow of her head.

"You appear to have another fan, Kort. Perhaps you should make sure she doesn't have an influential father."

We watch the server make her way back through the crowd dodging gropes.

"I really didn't know."

"Of course you didn't. I bet she wouldn't dodge if *you* reached for her."

"Maybe."

"I think she wants to play with your sword."

I chuckled. "Perhaps."

"Why did she call you a sword?"

"My homeland doesn't have Marines. They have Swords."

"I see." She took a drink of her wine and frowned.

She laid a finger against the side of the glass and muttered a single word that slipped right back out of my mind as quickly as I heard it. Frost formed on the side of the glass and her eyes glowed blue for a moment which faded over the next few seconds.

I felt the hair on the back of my neck raise.

She pointed at my glass of ale which I slid toward her she repeated the action. Frost formed on the side of my glass.

"I should have used fire after you got is posted in the Sable district."

I sipped the ice cold ale. "It sure is a lot better cold."

"Indeed." She sipped her wine again. "We are to report tomorrow in Sable. I really have much better wine at home. I will see you tomorrow morning."

She stood and walked straight toward the door. There were no groping hands and everyone stepped out of her way. Angering a sorceress was probably one of the most stupid things a fella could do.

I reached across the table and pulled her wine back to my side.

"Waste not, want not," I muttered. I drank the sweet wine. "Still prefer ale. Mead would be preferable."

"No one in this godforsaken country can make Mead," the Fallanasi woman said as she stepped back to the table. "My shift is over in a moment. The drinks are a silver."

I pulled two silvers from my pouch and handed them to her. "The other is for you."

"Thank you, my Lord."

"Just a Marine," I said.

"Tell yourself what you must, my Lord. I was a girl in Tyranis when the Swords held the gates. Halcyon brought his hordes. One hundred and thirty-two Swords held the gates against thousands. Call yourself *just* a Marine if you will."

For a moment I was lost in the past surrounded by blood and death.

"Where did you go, my Lord."

"Just the past."

"Perhaps you would join me in the present and we can forget the past for a while."

"Perhaps."

CHAPTER TWO

I strapped the pair of swords around my waist admiring the naked woman sleeping on the bed. I slipped out the door quietly so she could sleep and made my way down the stairs and out the front door of Boggan's.

"She *did* want to play with your sword," Serafine said as I stepped out the door.

"Perhaps. Her name is Alicia."

"You weren't at the barracks so I figured I'd find you here."

"I guess we should go face the music," I said. "Sable is going to suck though."

"Undoubtedly."

We turned east and began walking toward Sable district. Sable was one district away from the warehouse district. The north comprised the docks which were a handful in themselves. Just below the docks was the heart of the Sable district. Taverns, bordellos, restaurants, and any number of other shops filled the area and were frequented by the sailors when they were in port.

To the east of the Sable district was the warehouse district so there were always convoys from the docks to the warehouses that needed extra protection. We were in the High District at the moment which held the Rhymen Marine barracks.

We would travel through Merrick and Parch before we reached Sable. Some districts were named after the ruling class. Merrick had been a general in the Army during the Rhymen invasion of the Toulondi Peninsula. Parch was a noble family in the old days of Rhyme.

There was noise ahead.

"Of course we can't have a peaceful stroll to our next assignment," Serafine said.

"Not likely."

We turned a corner and took in the scene ahead of us. The square was crowded with people yelling at a figure floating in the air above them.

"Sorcerer," I muttered.

"It's almost like you don't like sorcery," she said. "I really don't understand why."

"Really?"

"Oh, you mean because of Tarl Redmane?"

"Maybe. He *did* set me on fire."

"I seem to remember you relieved him of his hands for that."

"Hard to cast spells as a ritualist without hands."

"This is true. Evokers use their voices." She motioned toward the floating man. "This one seems to use talismans."

"You can tell that from back here?"

"There are no words of power being spoken. His flight is powered by that medallion around his neck. His behavior is powered by that bottle in his hand."

"I don't doubt that."

The man floating above the crowd dropped something that flashed with a loud pop. The people nearby scrambled away from it holding their ears.

"Flash bang." My hand rested on my sword.

"He hasn't hurt anyone yet. Perhaps he can keep his hands?"

"Maybe."

She strode forward into the crowd which parted before her as soon as they saw her white hair and Marine tabard. I followed with a hand on my sword. She focused on the floating sorcerer while my focus stayed on the crowd around us. Magic was her purview.

The floating sorcerer laughed, reached into his bag, and dropped another of his talismans.

Serafine spoke one of those words that slipped into and out of my mind and the talisman sailed skyward to explode next to the sorcerer who grabbed his own ears.

His head jerked to the side to stare at Serafine when the word of power slipped in and out of his mind.

She pointed toward the ground.

He shook his head and reached for the bag.

She muttered another word and the amulet around his neck glowed for a moment before dissolving to dust. He fell to the ground 20 feet below.

"Good one," I said.

"Talismans," she muttered in disgust.

"You know *we* use talismans," I said.

"I have no need of them."

I grinned and followed her toward the fallen sorcerer who no longer held the bottle or a talisman. He was too busy holding his leg which was bent in the wrong direction.

"You broke my leg you…"

"Finish that sentence wond it may be your last," I said with my hand on my sword. "When you are given an order by a Marine, do it."

"It was just harmless fun," he whined.

"Just be glad it was her." I pointed toward

Serafine. "The last sorcerer I brought in lost his hands."

His right hand strayed toward his bag and my sword flashed into my hand faster than the eye could see.

"I suppose you could still lose one."

His hand stopped.

"That might be the smartest thing you've done all day," Serafine said. "He's not kidding. He doesn't like sorcerers and Redmane was a pretty powerful one."

"Grisham's Ghost! You're *that* Marine?"

I shrugged. "Remove the bag slowly and lay it on the ground. You even look like you're reaching inside of it… Well, you can figure that out."

"Y…Yes sir."

"Sorcerers," I muttered under my breath.

"I'll try not to take any offense."

"You're different. You're my partner."

She muttered a word of power and the bag was surrounded by a glowing nimbus.

"Is there anything else in your pockets?"

He shook his head.

"She's going to search you if she even winces I'm going to plant this sword through your left eye."

"You know, I think there might be a couple of coins…"

CHAPTER THREE

Every district has its own holding cells some districts only have a few Marines stationed at them but all of them have at least a small compound. That compound may be a building or a city block depending on the district. Merrick had a single building with sixteen Marines assigned.

We left the errant sorcerer in their care and continued east into the Parch District. Merrick was comprised mostly of domiciles for the middle class. Parch was mostly working class housing.

"More crowded," Serafine said.

"Yeah but I don't see any floating sorcerers."

"True enough," she responded. "I've seen three pickpockets and a couple that might be casing a shop."

"Seven pickpockets and those two are

definitely casing that shop. I'll be back in a second."

"Magical wards," I said a few moments later from behind the two. "Not worth the trouble."

They both turned around quickly, eyes widening as they recognize the tabard.

"Not interested in arresting you," I said. "But I know you now. These people are working class not going to have enough to make it worth your while."

"I don't know what you're talking about." The taller of the two shrugged.

"That's okay I'll tell them that when they remove your hands. Thievery has consequences. Have a nice day."

I walked back to join Serafine.

"What did you tell them?"

"Thievery has consequences."

"What is it with you and hands?"

"People don't get into near as much trouble if they don't have hands."

"They also can't wipe their ass."

"That doesn't help with the smell," I said. "But consequences are consequences."

She shook her head. "You, my friend, have issues."

"You have no idea."

"One guy sets you on fire and now you want to cut everybody's hands off."

"Not everybody's."

"A lot more than before it happened."

I shrugged. "You get set on fire and see if it doesn't change your outlook."

"Hard pass."

"Understandable," I said. "It's not something you choose to do. No one in their right mind chooses to be set on fire."

"If I'd been there it wouldn't have happened."

"You were playing around in the square. That thing with the necromancer."

"I hate necromancers," she said in disgust.

"Seems like that would be a messy skill to have."

"Extremely messy."

"Can you…?"

"I can but refuse to do it. There are consequences to using dark magic. Much better to use the light of Khiron to counter it."

"Everybody said it was pretty impressive," I said. "I was busy being set on fire, so I missed it."

"You're just not going to let that go, are you?"

"Some things are just hard to forget."

"The Priestess healed you up perfectly fine. The goddess Shalira smiled on you that day. She doesn't choose to heal everyone. You were doing the work of the gods"

"Still hurt like a bitch." I caught a scent and stopped in my tracks. "That smells divine."

"Smells like pork," she said.

"What say we eat lunch before we report in."

"Our orders didn't specify any particular time today," she said motioning toward the stall for the enticing smell was coming from. "Shall we?"

CHAPTER FOUR

"What in the world did you do to get sent here?"

Serafine stepped aside so I could enter.

"Oh," the sergeant frowned. "Him."

"What?" I looked around. "What did I do?"

"I think it was more a matter of who," he said. "I'm Sergeant Donovan, third shift head of the watch. Everyone is quite familiar with who *you* offended."

"I didn't know."

"Did you ask?"

"That's not really a question you ask in a situation like that."

"That's the *first* question you ask in a situation like that, Marine."

"I bet you didn't ask your girl, Alicia, did you?" Serafine smirked.

I shook my finger at her. "That's not fair."

She chuckled.

"Far be it from me to look a gift horse in the mouth, though," the sergeant said. "Two investigators added to my roster are always welcome. We have several open cases that haven't been assigned yet."

He pushed three files across his desk. "Pick one, pick two, hells, take all three. Knock yourself out. Get to work."

Serafine grinned and walked by me out of the office. I picked up the folders and followed her.

"Always ask, Marine," Donovan said, shaking his head.

"I guess everybody's heard about it," I muttered as I followed Serafine into the bullpen.

There were a number of desks in the bullpen that were occupied by other detectives, several of which were eyeballing Serafine speculatively.

I guess I couldn't blame them. Women were scarce in the Marines and she was beautiful with her northern features. Most of the gazes ended when they took in the snow white hair. She kept her hood raised most of the time which hid her short-cut white hair but some of it always seem to slip out of the hooded darkness.

She motioned toward a pair of empty desks in the corner. "Are these free?"

"Go for it," a large redheaded man said. His features made me think of the Western lands of Tampril.

In Rhyme you would see almost every race of man collected within the city walls.

She took a seat and I slid the chair from the neighboring desk across from her. She handed me a leather folder.

I removed my swords, leaned them against the desk, and sat down.

"This one looks like possible extortion," I said as I read the initial statements.

"Got a murder here," she said. "I don't think it's been very high in the rank of importance."

"Why is that?"

"Pleasure girl."

"They do tend to get kicked to the bottom," I said. "High risk profession."

"I want this one," she said.

"I expect so. Slide me that other one."

I open the folder and read the opening. "Robbery."

"What do you think?" She asked.

"Murder takes highest priority," I said. "Let's look at that one first."

"Agreed. Says she was cut up pretty badly and left in an alley."

"I guess we should go speak to the resident coroner." I turned to look at the red-headed Marine. "Who's the local coroner?"

"We have a thaumaturge in the basement. Name's Gareth. He's a little weird, but most thaumaturges are a little weird."

"Potions," Serafine grumbled.

"Do you like anyone who's not an evoker?"

"I don't like most evokers either."

I looked back at the other investigator. "Thanks…"

"Simms."

"Thanks, Simms." I held my hand out. "I'm Kort."

He grasped my hand. "Most of us already know who you are, Kort."

"Doesn't surprise me," I said. "I'm guessing it's not for the reasons I would prefer to be known."

"That depends," he said. "You prefer being known for taking down Redmane, or that you took down a certain officer's daughter?"

I picked up the folder and my swords. "That's going to follow me around isn't it?"

He grinned. "More than likely."

Serafine was barely containing laughter.

I pointed at her. "I don't need anything out of you."

She snorted and strode toward the door.

I followed her out the door and around the side of the building where the entrance to the basement was located. I slung my sword belt over my shoulder and followed her down the ramp to a set of double doors.

There was an odd smell coming from the doors.

"Potions," Serafine grumbled once more. "Try not to breathe too deeply."

She muttered a word of power and a slight glow covered the bottom half of her face. Then she walked through the door.

"I don't need a magic filter," I muttered. "Thanks for offering."

The smells were a lot stronger when I stepped inside. Layers and layers of fragrances that I assumed were used to disguise the scent of death underneath.

I wasn't sure what I expected the coroner to look like but I didn't expect a 5 foot tall bald-headed man with a beard that hung almost to his waist. I was used to the coroner in the high district who was almost the exact opposite of this fellow.

"What can I do you for?" The small man asked. "You must be the new investigators. No one else comes down here anymore. I usually have to take my reports up to them. I'm Small."

"I know," Serafine replied. "Rather obvious."

He laughed. "My name is Gareth Small. I like to see the reactions when I introduce myself."

I chuckled and handed him the folder on the pleasure girl. "We picked up this case. We'd like to see the body."

"Oh, this one's already shipped out. Can't keep them down here very long."

"I was hoping we had gotten here before that," I said.

"You can probably still catch her before they put her in the cemetery. She just went out about an hour ago."

"All right," I said. "We'll try to catch them and then come back and talk to you."

"Not much I will be able to add to the report. She was stabbed. Cut up pretty badly. Whoever did this continued cutting her long after she was dead. There was a lot of rage in this."

"Damn." I took the folder he extended back toward me.

"We'll be in touch if we have any further questions, Mister Small." Serafine said.

"I'll be here."

I followed Serafine out the door and back up the ramp. "You still want to see the body?"

"We probably should," she replied.

"Then I'd say we better hit the bricks if we plan to get there before they put her in the ground. They usually don't waste any time."

"I bet it's late enough they wait till the morning."

"I guess it depends on how ripe the body is."

"True enough. Shall I make a door?"

"You know I hate those things."

"That's part of the fun," she said. "Just don't listen to them."

"It's really hard not to listen."

She shrugged and uttered three words of power that slid from my mind as quickly as I heard them.

"Stupid doors," I muttered. As I followed her into the glowing Nimbus that appeared in front of us.

I kept my focus on her back and followed her to the glowing spot on the other end of the tunnel. Voices assailed my senses. They ranged from pleading for help to screaming and there were thousands of them all speaking at once. We stepped through the other side.

"I hate those things," I muttered. "It's like walking through the hells."

"I know." She grinned.

"Asshole."

CHAPTER FIVE

I could still hear the voices echoing in my head as we walked through the cemetery gates.

The box wagon used for carrying bodies through the city was parked alongside the building at the far left side of the property. The horse was still connected to the wagon so it couldn't have been there long.

"Looks like we probably made it in time," Serafine said.

"I still hate using the doors."

We walked down the pathway to the mortuary, where people had one last chance to see their loved ones before they were buried.

We were met at the door by a black robed priest.

"Are you here to see a loved one?" He asked.

"Not really," I said. "We need to see a recently arrived body. Vivian Lorette."

"I'm sorry, Vivian Lorette has already been buried."

"Bullshit."

I glanced over at Serafine.

"He's lying," she said.

"You know it doesn't pay to lie to a Marine," I said. "I suggest you take me to the body."

"I can't."

Serafine uttered a word and the priest staggered backwards.

"Blasphemer!" He cringed. "I am a priest of Gairestis!"

"One who cannot lie to me again," she said. "Where is the body?"

"I… I don't know."

"That's not good at all," I said. "Why don't you know?"

"The body disappeared almost as soon as it arrived here."

I could tell he didn't want to say any of the words he was saying which led me to believe Serafine's spell was working correctly.

"Why did you lie to us to begin with?" I asked. "When something like that occurs you're supposed to report it to the Marines. We are the Marines."

"Th…There have been others."

"Shit."

"Pleasure girls?" Serafine asked.

He shook his head.

"You're about to put together a list for me," she said. "I want names, genders, professions… Every detail."

He nodded quickly.

"Some priest," I said in disgust. "Gairestis deserves better."

He started to bluster but stopped. It could've been Serafine's spell or it just might have been the way my left eye was twitching and the way my right hand rested on the hilt of my sword.

Gairestis was a god of the downtrodden. His doctrine was peace, charity, and mercy.

At least I think it was. There were so many gods it was hard to keep track.

He hurried back into the mortuary to fetch our list.

"Now I have to wonder if it's connected. Does our killer come back and take the bodies?" I mused.

"We'll know more when we have the list," she said. "We can follow up with each district on the cases if we need to."

"If they're not connected to the killings and I'm afraid something really bad is going on."

"It screams of necromancy," she said with an icy tone.

"Necromancy, necrophilia… I'm pretty sure anything that starts with necro is going to be bad." I was looking at the black strands in the colors of her eyes. "Is it something you're familiar with?"

"Necromancy is dark sorcery. I have the ability but I will never delve into it."

"Might be nice to wake someone up and ask him who killed them."

"When you open that door, you can't close it back. Those voices you hear when we walk through the dimensions? Imagine hearing them all the time… everywhere."

"Nevermind then. I don't want to hear them for the few seconds it takes to walk through the doors. Is that why necromancers are bat shit crazy?"

"My guess is it plays a very large part. It's easier for a necromancer to be a talismanic. Everything stays connected to the talisman. For an Evoker…" She shuddered.

"He actually came back," I said as the priest returned with a scroll in his hand.

"He is terrified, not stupid."

"Sometimes terror is worse than stupidity," I said.

"True enough."

"Th…There are ten missing bodies," the priest stammered.

"When did it start?" I asked.

"Four days ago."

"Four days and you didn't inform the Marines?"

"There were rumors of a group of Tolers down in the undercroft. At first I thought it might be them. With the loss of the three bodies that arrived today, I would have reported."

I looked toward Serafine to see her nod. The truth spell was still working so the man couldn't lie.

"These are three different districts," I said. "When we leave here I expect you to report to the other two."

"Most certainly."

"If you don't, Gairestis will be short a priest. Understand?"

He nodded quickly.

Serafine took the scroll and I followed her out the door.

"Tolers my ass," I muttered. "Even Tolers forgo their normal cuisine when they're in Rhyme. Most people are uncomfortable with carrion eaters."

"Just looking at the scroll tells me this is a bigger problem than someone preying on pleasure girls. We do have someone killing girls, but I don't think the disappearing bodies have anything to do with that. Two of the names on this list were pleasure girls, one from Sabre, the other from the Market District."

"Reckon we need to walk to the Market District headquarters and talk to whoever's investigating it. Which makes me a lot happier because it's between here and Sable."

"Why does that make you happier?"

"None of your damned dimensional doors."

She chuckled.

CHAPTER SIX

We walked out the gates and I glanced back at the enormous cemetery. It was probably as large as the Market District. They tell me it used to be a little ways out of town in the old days, but Rhyme was a lot smaller then. If the city kept growing, I wondered how much they would reserve for the cemetery when it grew past it.

We turned north along Temple Row. Temple Row had become its own district with all of the temples of the various gods. It seemed like there was a new one every year. Say what you want about the Rhymen Empire, but they never forced any religion upon anyone. When they brought a new country into the Empire, they took any of the features that they could use and left the rest.

"That's a new one," I said pointing at a small temple.

"It's hard to keep up with all the names," she said. "But I think that one is Hartness."

"I haven't heard of that one."

"Something to do with scribes," she said. "I can't remember the exact nature. Now I'm going to have to look it up. Thank you, I needed more work to do."

"You don't have to look it up. There will be three more next week."

"Yeah."

Part of what made Serafine such a good detective was the fact that she couldn't go without finding answers. Something popped into her head and she would have to find the answer or it would plague her. It did make her a great detective. Not so pleasant for those around her sometimes.

In Fallanasi, I had a friend who raised bloodhounds. When they got the scent of something they would follow it to the ends of the realms if you would let them.

Serafine was similar when something intrigued her.

I had a feeling the disappearing bodies was going to be something like that. I agreed with her in that I didn't think the pleasure girls' killer had anything to do with the disappearing bodies. I couldn't swear to that but it just didn't feel like it was connected.

My guess was we just inherited a new case to go with the others.

"I have a feeling there's not going to be much sleep in the near future."

"Quite possible."

The Marines at Temple Gate waved as they saw our tabards. Rhyme had grown well past its walls over the years.

"You think they will start a new wall this year?" I asked as we walked through the gate.

"I almost think the days of walls for Rhyme might be over."

"You think?"

"Look at the size of the Empire. I'm not sure there's anyone out there who can rival it."

"There are."

"You sound quite sure."

"You sound like someone who was raised in Rhyme."

She chuckled. "You could be right."

"The Solgothi would be one of them."

"Why would they come here?" She asked with one eyebrow raised. "They would have to sail across the Kaliban Sea with legions of soldiers."

"I'm just saying they could."

"True enough."

The market district began right after the gate but the Marine post was over near Westgate so we turned left and walked down the street beside the wall. On our right was shop after shop after shop. If you wanted to buy something it was available in the market district. Well, most things. The other things were available in Sable.

Not that you can't buy some of those things in the market district. They were just disguised a little better. For instance, the large two-story shop we were passing was a house of pleasure girls. Several were sitting on the upstairs balcony and there was little doubt as to their profession.

"You think the other girl might have come from there?" I asked.

"It's possible. Should we stop and ask?"

"The Marines would know for certain but it probably wouldn't hurt to ask. It might save walking back over here after we talk to the Marines."

"Agreed."

We were met as we entered by a tall older woman wearing a dress that looked to be Lillian silk. She was still beautiful even with the years.

"Marines," she bowed her head. "Marines are always welcome. Is this business or pleasure?"

"Business," Serafine said. "We just happened across a case that involved a girl from this district and we were curious whether any of you would be familiar with her. Her name was Dali Meere."

"Of course we know Dali. She is upstairs."

"What?"

"She was with a client earlier today. She is due to wake in an hour or so for the evening shift."

"We must have been mistaken. The girl we are looking for was murdered." I pointed at the scroll. "It seems she was misidentified. Sorry to bother you."

"Marines are usually a little bit more careful than that," Serafine said as we stepped out the door. "Perhaps we should wake the girl and interview her."

"The Madame didn't seem to be lying."

"True. I suppose we'll find out when we get to the Marine post. It was either shoddy work or something…"

"What?"

"Something just feels off."

"Agreed."

"I guess we should talk to the Marines first. We'll come back and talk to the girl if necessary." She turned right and continued down the street.

Throngs of people filled the street but they seem to part as she got near them. That's why I tended to follow behind her. Sorcery made a lot of people nervous and her white hair was hard to miss with her hood down. People just naturally wanted to get out of her way, whether she wore the tabard or not.

Also I didn't have to focus on the crowds ahead of us so I could watch the sides without worrying about walking into someone. This was what allowed me to see the hooded figure in the alley just as he threw his blade.

The world seemed to slow as I stepped forward and snatched the blade from the air, spun around, and let it fly back to its source.

It had been aimed at Serafine.

My eyes roved the area in search of more attackers. The crowds in the street still hadn't registered what had happened. The scream from the hooded figure in the alley ended that. He staggered forward from the alley with the hilt of his own knife protruding from his neck.

His hand grabbed the hilt and pulled.

"Bad idea," I muttered as blood arced from the artery the blade had been blocking.

In moments he was face down in the street.

A word of power slipped through my mind as Serafine cast a spell and a glowing nimbus formed around her.

"That's alright," I said. "I don't need a glowy shield thingy."

The crowd was scrambling for cover with no idea the fight was already over. It seemed odd that a single person would attack a pair of Marines but it seemed that was the case.

Another word of power slid through my mind.

"There are no others," she said. "At least none with ill intent toward us."

"Good," I said and approached the body.

I removed the hood.

"I don't recognize him," I said. "You?"

"I don't. But there's something dark."

I opened one of his eyes. "No dark threads and the hair is natural, not dyed."

"Something just feels off," she said.

"Could just be because he threw a knife at you."

"It could." She pointed to the crowd. "Leave the body as it is. We'll send someone for it."

CHAPTER SEVEN

"We'll send one of the rookies to fetch the body," the sergeant said. "Have you got any idea why they were targeting you?"

"I have no idea. We're stationed in Sable." I said. "I'm not sure why someone would be targeting us in Market."

"Then I have to ask, why are you in Market?"

"We were following a lead. Recently we had a pleasure girl murdered. According to a list from the cemetery you had a pleasure girl murdered here as well. Plus we've heard some troubling news about bodies disappearing including the girl from here and the one from Sable."

"Disappearing bodies?"

"Yes. Ten, at the moment. They were

shipped to the mortuary. Sometime between then and their burial the bodies disappeared."

"I think I know which case you're talking about with the pleasure girl. Dali Meere."

"That's the name, but we stopped at a pleasure house on the way here and they say Dali is alive and well. I thought, perhaps, we could talk to the investigator about the identification."

"Cobb was the investigator," the sergeant said. "He should be back in the office within the hour. His shift starts soon."

"Good," I said. "Do you have any sorcerers working this district?"

"We have one fire sorceress. Vina Kor."

"My guess is she was the target. White hair, female Marine."

"That makes more sense than I want it to," he said. "I'll send a couple of Marines to her place."

Serafine and I stood to leave the office.

"One question, Marine."

I turned back to the sergeant. "What?"

"How in the Hells did you catch that dagger?"

I grinned and walked out of the office.

"It's a good question," Serafine said. "I've never seen you do anything like that before."

"No one's ever thrown a dagger at us.

There are a lot of things I can do you've never seen."

"Is that so?"

I shrugged. "Let's go to one of the local spots and get some dinner. We can wait until Cobb shows up."

"That sounds like a plan," she said. "Perhaps they'll have some fresh vegetables."

"Not out of the question this time of year." I stepped out the front door of the outpost. "Pheasant would be nice. Or even a fat chicken."

"I'll stick with the vegetables," she said.

"That's fine. More for me."

She shook her head as we crossed the street toward a shop that smelled delightful.

Cobb showed up at the shop about thirty minutes after we sat down and the sergeant sent him over. He looked to be in his thirties and a little bit heavyset. The axe on his back told me more than anything about the man at first sight. I guessed his heavyset frame concealed a lot of muscle. It takes a lot of muscle to swing a battleax for any length of time.

He saw us immediately as he stepped in the room and hesitated. Then he made his way over to our table where I was just finishing off a chicken. Serafine was delicately cutting pieces of vegetables and eating them.

"I'm guessing you're the two from Sable," Cobb said as he stopped beside the table.

I motioned toward the chair. "Have a seat."

"The boss said you had something on Meere?" He asked as he pulled the ax from his back and leaned it against the wall next to my swords.

"According to the madame at the pleasure house Meere was asleep upstairs when we came through. Is there any chance you misidentified the body?"

"Did you go up and see the girl?"

"We didn't, but I'm not sure it would have made any difference if we did since we don't know what she looked like anyway. Have you met her in person?"

"I have."

"If you get the opportunity, you might want to go see if it is her."

"So what has you checking on the status of pleasure girls in the market district?"

"We caught a case in Sable of a pleasure girl who was cut up pretty badly," Serafine said. "The coroner had already sent the body to the mortuary so we went to examine it before it got buried. When we got there we discovered the body was missing along with several more that have disappeared over the last week including one Dali Meere."

"Missing bodies?"

She placed the scroll in front of him. "Ten of them."

He looked over the names on the scroll. "Three of those came from here."

"That's why we came through here on our way back to Sable." I pointed toward the scroll with the chicken leg I was eating.

"I see. I'll definitely check into these. I appreciate you stopping through."

"If you find anything, can you send a messenger? The description of the way the girl was cut up is similar to the one from our district. Not sure if the disappearing bodies has anything to do with that but I think maybe the same person killed the two girls."

"Did she have a star cut into her heel?"

"According to the coroner, she did."

"So did Dali."

"So they're definitely connected," she said. "That's a signature."

"But what connection do they have to the others on this list?" He rolled the scroll back up and handed it to Serafine.

"We have no idea yet," she said. "But we're going to be digging into that when we get back to Sable."

"I'll see if I can find a connection between the three of these and I'll check on Dali. If the body we found wasn't her, it was someone who looked an awful lot like her. It's not something I thought I could mistake."

"You *knew* her," she said.

"Yes. If she's alive, you have no idea how relieved I'll be."

"I hope she's alive, for your sake. If she is though, we'll need to figure out who the other girl was and that's going to be hard to do with no body."

"True." Cobb stood. "I'm going to take a walk down the road and see if it's her. I'll send a messenger your way as soon as I find out."

CHAPTER EIGHT

"He knew her."

"Do I detect a little bit of disgust?" I asked.

"Man taking advantage of a woman…"

"Perhaps it was simply a man paying for something the woman was selling. There's nothing wrong with that on his part or hers."

"You don't think that woman tried something else before she had to become a pleasure girl?"

"I have no idea." I shrugged. "Maybe she did, maybe she chose that job because she enjoys it. I don't know her so I can't make that judgment until I do. You don't know her, do you?"

"I don't."

"Seems you're rushing to a judgment without all the evidence."

She frowned. "You're right."

"I've seen women forced into a profession they don't want but have also seen the other end of the spectrum. I know a woman who spent ten years as a pleasure girl before retiring and buying her own villa. She went into the business specifically to achieve that goal. She had something to sell that was in demand and she controlled how she sold it."

"And how often does that happen?"

"Probably a lot more often than you think," I said. "Here in Rhyme, I'm not sure what the ratio is. I've seen both here. I've only been working here for a little over a year."

"I've lived in Rhyme my whole life," she said. "It sounds like your country might be a little nicer."

"On some levels, yes."

"You don't talk about your home much, Kort." She lifted her wine and motioned toward me. "We see a lot of people in Rhyme, but very few of your people."

"There will be more in time. Until recently, my people were forbidden to leave. With the death of the Archon, a new age has begun. I was surprised when I met Alicia yesterday but I expect more in the future. We've all heard of the great Rhymen Empire."

"I've learned more about you in the last few seconds than I have in the whole year since you became my partner."

"You've never really asked before."

"I haven't?"

"Nope."

"Then I suppose it's my own fault," she said. "Until yesterday, I had no idea they called you a Sword. What kind of duties does a sword have?"

"We fought for the Archon." I took a long drink of the ale in front of me. "Sword of Fallanasi, chosen of the Three…"

"I feel there is a larger story there," she said. "That bittersweet tone."

"The Swords are no more. Our order was disbanded. Most of them joined the new Fallanasi Guard. The new counsel do not follow the Three. I suppose if you live long enough, you become obsolete."

"Yet you're here in Rhyme working as a Marine. Which is basically the same as the Guard?"

"Rhyme did not require me to break any oaths. The Archon is gone but the Three remain. I chose to leave rather than forswear my oaths to the Three."

"I see."

I shrugged. "Don't get me wrong. I'm not a priest or a monk."

"I figured that with your proclivities."

I chuckled and finished off my ale. "Unless I was a priest of Madrigal."

"True enough. Madrigal, the God of pleasure."

"The problem is people get pleasure from a lot of different things and I'm not certain Madrigal worries about where the pleasure comes from."

"I think you're right."

"It happens occasionally."

"It's too rare for me not to admit it when it happens."

I grunted. "Asshole."

She laughed. "Let's get out of here. It's late enough, I doubt we'll get any more work done today. I think I'll go home."

"No barracks for you, huh?"

"I think they prefer it if I don't stay in the barracks. Most Marines are nervous around me."

"Probably."

"Meet you at the barracks in the morning?"

"I'm thinking about going back to Boggan's."

"She must've been really nice."

I grinned. "She is."

"Then I'll stop by there and pick you up."

"See you then."

I watched as she stood, paid for our dinners, and walked out the door. In moments I followed her. She walked north toward the high district and I followed at a distance. Boggan's Tavern was in the high district too. I wanted to keep an eye on Serafine after the attempt on her life.

I felt the word of power slide through my mind.

She turned to look at me.

I chuckled and walked forward.

"Why are you following me?"

"Guy threw a dagger at you earlier. Thought I would keep my eye on you till you got home."

"I have been walking these streets for the last eight years, Kort."

"How many times has someone thrown a dagger at you?" I asked.

She shrugged. "Perhaps you have a point. Would you feel better if I raise a shield?"

"Probably."

"Then I will." She pointed to the street on our right. "Boggan's is that way."

I chuckled. "All right."

Another word of power and the slightly glowing Nimbus formed around her. "This will stop anything."

I nodded and turned right. It still took all of my willpower not to follow her. I worried about her, Sometimes she lived in her own world. I was her partner and it was my job to watch her back. I didn't know exactly where she lived, although I knew it was in the high district where many nobles lived.

Her family may have been servants for the nobles but it was doubtful. I had a sneaky suspicion they were part of the wealthy. Serafine always had coin, I never really questioned why.

As she had said before it's probably my own fault that I didn't know any more about her than I did. I had never asked and neither had she. We just went to work and did our jobs.

CHAPTER NINE

The sky was darkening as I reached Boggan's Tavern. It wasn't all from night falling, a strong scent of rain filled the air.

"Oh great," I muttered. "Maybe it'll be through by morning. Nothing like traipsing around in the rain…"

Alicia waved from the far side of the Tavern as I stepped in the door. She was a small piece of familiar in a strange place and I enjoyed her company greatly.

I sat at the same table I was at before with my back to the wall. Alicia crossed the room to place a tankard of ale in front of me and stooped over to kiss me. There were a few catcalls and whistles.

"Busy night," she said with a smile. "I'll be back."

Her trip back across the room was much

easier without having to dodge groping hands. There were still a couple but nowhere near what I had seen as she approached the table. Whether it was just respect to another Marine or not was unknown. One of the Marines was quietly chastised by an older Marine.

I heard the name Redmane more than one time.

"Who is Redmane?" Alicia asked when she returned to the table.

"Sorcerer we had a problem with."

"One of them said you cut his hands off."

"I did." I took a drink from my tankard. "Ritualist. Hard for them to cast spells without hands."

"I was prepared to meet a variety of people when I left home. The number of sorcerers in Rhyme still astound me."

"It surprised me as well. But I discovered that not all sorcerers are bent on death and destruction."

"Your partner?"

"She's one of the good ones."

"Will you be staying tonight?"

"If you want me to."

"Of course I want you to." She smiled again.

Several hours later I soaked in a large tub of steaming water.

"That talisman is very handy," she said

pointing at the crystal hanging next to my swords. "Keeping hot water for any length of time is usually impossible."

"The Marines have a talismanic that works for them. She keeps us supplied in various talismans to use for our jobs. That one has another official use but it makes a good water heater."

"It does."

Unfastening the dress she wore, it fell to the floor and she stepped over the edge into the tub.

"I was pleasantly surprised when you returned this evening. It's not typical of a Sword."

"I'm still learning what it means to be free," I said. "Swords are forbidden to make attachments. I enjoyed our night and there was no one telling me whether or not I could come back and see you again. No one except you, of course."

She settled in front of me and laid back against my chest in the tub. "I enjoyed our night as well. Perhaps we'll spend a few more nights together. Perhaps many."

My arms encircled her. "I think I would like that."

CHAPTER TEN

I strapped my swords on and picked up the talisman. Looking at it for a moment, I placed it on the stand beside the bed. Knowing I could return was a strange thing for me. *Wanting* to return was an even stranger feeling.

It seemed Rhyme was corrupting me.

"But is it really corruption?" I muttered as I stepped out into the street, my eyes constantly moving.

It seemed the rain had moved on around Rhyme without dropping more than a few sprinkles. The cobblestones were dry.

I recognized Serafine as she was striding down the center of the street as if she owned it.

I chuckled. "Definitely a noble."

I waved and stepped in alongside when she reached me.

"I guess she enjoyed your sword," she said. "Two nights in a row. Where is my partner? What have you done with him?"

"He's still here."

"I'm wondering."

I shrugged.

"In the year that I've known you, you've been with a number of women but you never went back a second night with any of them."

"I like her."

"Then I like her too. Let's go to work."

"Maybe we'll have a peaceful—"

"Don't even say it," she interrupted. "You're not going to jinx this."

"You have a point."

I followed Serafine down the crowded street. She had dropped her hood and the crowd seemed to split as she approached. Most people gave sorcerers a wide berth.

As we reached the Merrick district, I smelled a wonderful scent.

Serafine caught the smell as well and came to a halt. "That smells like sticky buns."

"You know we have to find them now," I said.

We followed our noses to a shop on the left side of the street where a short, rotund baker was placing sticky buns in rows on his display.

"I'd like to get a couple of those," I said as I stepped forward.

He turned. "Marines. I don't recognize you though."

"We're stationed over a few districts." I motioned down the street. "I didn't see you out here yesterday."

"Some crazy sorcerer was out terrorizing people so I stayed in the shop." He nodded to Serafine. "No offense intended."

"None taken," she said. "The guy was drunk and an asshole."

"Oh," he said in realization. "You two are the ones who arrested him."

She nodded.

He took down a paper bag and filled it with sticky buns. It held seven.

"These are for the good work you did yesterday." He handed the bag to Serafine. "No charge. You did us all a service."

"Thank you," she answered.

"You two enjoy those. They are from a recipe my mother passed down to me."

Serafine handed me one of the buns and I took a bite.

"These are magnificent, sir."

"They are much easier to make now since we are able to buy the Fallanasi honey legally." He motioned toward me. "I would say you know this quite well already. We don't see many Fallanasi here in Rhyme."

"Most people don't recognize us," I said after I swallowed the bite of sticky bun. "I'm usually asked a couple times a day where I'm from."

"The best honey comes from Fallanasi."

"I won't argue that. I wouldn't mind getting some of it, myself."

"Perhaps we can set something up," he said. "My next shipment comes next week."

"We can definitely set something up," I said and stuffed the rest of the sticky bun in my mouth.

I glanced at Serafine who was just watching quietly as she devoured buns.

"How many of those have you already eaten?"

She shrugged and grabbed another one from the bag before handing it to me.

I looked inside at the single sticky bun at the bottom and then back at Serafine who had a drip of honey on the side of her mouth.

"Five?"

She grinned and took another bite.

CHAPTER ELEVEN

"I may have to create doors to get to work from now on." Serafine sat down at the desk. "If we have to pass that shop every morning, I'll end up as big as a house."

"You didn't have to eat five," I said.

"Oh, but I did. You're lucky you got any of them. That honey was divine, like eating sweet sunshine."

"It's from the naranga blossoms," I said. "You can't beat naranga blossom honey."

"Naranga?"

"I would say it won't be long before we're seeing them in the markets. Fallanasi has spent years combining the best naranga to grow the sweetest fruit. They are unmistakable when you see them. They are round and have a thick orange peel. Actually the latest crop should be being harvested this month. I would say by this time next month there will be some here in Rhyme."

"Is the fruit as sweet as the honey?"

"Not as sweet as honey, there's not much that is. But they are a very sweet fruit and I believe they'll ship well. We also have a yellow fruit that is very similar in texture but is very sour. Narasta make a magnificent drink when mixed with water and honey."

"Interesting," she said and stood up. "I look forward to trying them. I'm going to report to Donovan what we found out so far."

"I'll look into this extortion thing so we can go out and talk to them today. Perhaps we can shake the trees a little bit and see what falls out about the murder while we're out there."

"Sounds like a plan. I'll be right back."

It looks like the extortion victim was new to Rhyme. He had set up less than two months ago at his father's old bread shop. His complaint was about someone demanding protection money.

"He couldn't be that stupid," I muttered.

"You overestimate humankind, Kort."

Serafine was back.

"I think this guy just reported the Uncrowned Prince for extortion."

"That's not very smart," she said.

"I agree. Although if it's not the Prince, someone else is trying to move in on the Prince. That could spell all kinds of trouble."

"We definitely need to go check this one out," she said. "We certainly don't need a war on the streets."

"I still don't understand this set up we have with the Prince but it was the first thing they told me when they hired me."

"The Prince is a necessary evil," she said as she looked through the folder I'd handed her. "You didn't see it before he took over. Crime was rampant. I remember as a little girl how scary the streets were. They say he was a beggar child who grew up on the streets. Over the years he made himself more important to the various criminals. After he took charge of the majority of the criminals in Rhyme he declared himself the Uncrowned Prince. Then he approached the Marines with his deal."

"The largest extortion scheme ever."

"True enough, but it works. Crime is kept to a minimum, pickpockets and thieves, mostly. We can focus on taking down more serious criminals."

"It's still a very strange set up."

She shrugged. "It was all set up before my time as a Marine. It's just part of the job, now."

"Until he goes too far I suppose," I said.

"In the eight years I've been with the Marines he hasn't. In fact, he's brought several criminals to us when they stepped over the line. Sometimes they were still living, sometimes not."

"Still seems to be a strange set up to me."

"It is what it is." She motioned toward the door. "Ready to go find out?"

"Sure," I said standing up to follow her out the door. "What did the Sergeant think about the disappearing bodies?"

"He gave us free rein to look into it. Said he would report it to all the other districts."

"Good. He seems competent enough. Wonder why he's stationed in Sable."

"Probably pissed off somebody higher up," she said. "I'm not sure anyone works this district because they want to."

"Everybody says it's a crap posting. At least three times as much criminal activity here than any other district."

"At least it shouldn't be boring."

"True enough," I said as we rounded a corner to walk south, deeper into Sable District.

There were yells ahead of us as the crowd parted for two figures grappling with one another.

"Definitely not boring," I said as I saw blades in their hands.

A word of power slipped through my mind and I grinned as the two forms forcibly separated. I kept my hand near the hilt of my sword in case it was necessary. Working with Serafine, it rarely was.

CHAPTER TWELVE

"Put these two in separate cells," Serafine said as we handed the two over to Bider, the large Toulondi who worked as the jailer. "They didn't have time for bloodshed. Kick them loose when they sober up."

"Will do," he said in an incredibly deep voice.

His huge hands settled on the two men and his fingers wrapped all the way around their necks as he steered them toward the back.

"Think they'll give him any trouble?" I asked with a grin.

"I would pay to see that."

"I can go tell them if you want. Enough gold, they probably will."

She looked thoughtful for a moment then shook her head. "I guess we just don't have time."

Simms, the redheaded Marine from

Tampril, was chuckling as I followed her back out the door.

"You think we'll make it more than 200 feet this time?" I asked.

"Not when you keep jinxing it." She pointed south where another crowd was forming around two struggling individuals.

"I'll take this one," Simms said as he stepped out the door behind us. He reached back and grabbed the battle axe just inside the door. "Do you think they'll resist?"

"One can hope," I said with a chuckle.

The large Marine strode forward through the crowd.

"He sounded very hopeful," Serafine said. "So violent. What is it with you weapon swingers? At least, maybe, he won't chop off their hands."

"It was just the one time," I grumbled.

"Was it though?" She asked and stepped into the street to head south. "It really seemed like you might have done that before."

"It was just the one time, here," I said and followed her keeping my eyes trained on Simms. I was fairly certain he wouldn't have any trouble as soon as they saw that enormous axe.

He looked disappointed when both men started backpedaling as soon as he stepped into the circle of people around them.

"Doesn't look like they're going to resist." I motioned back over my shoulder toward them with my thumb.

"They were just sailors, not idiots."

"True enough." I glanced back toward the docks. "Two ships in. Probably be plenty of fistfights while they're both in dock."

"Fistfights are okay," she said. "No blades."

"Knife fights are ugly."

"They are." She nodded. "I wonder of this bread merchant has sticky buns."

"I think you may have a problem," I said.

"I don't know what you're talking about."

I chuckled. "I smell bread so I know we're close."

"And I'm guessing that you're hungry again already?"

"I didn't eat five sticky buns."

"Five? There's no way I ate five. I'm sure you ate half of those."

"I almost lost a hand trying to get to the second one."

"The stories you tell," she said shaking her head. "There it is."

"Hmm. I don't see sticky buns out front."

"Pity."

We stepped inside the shop.

"It's about time someone showed up," the

pudgy baker said as he strode across the room toward us.

I held up a finger. "Before you go any further, I have a single question."

"What?"

"Have you paid the Prince?"

"I pay the Prince every week."

"Okay." I nodded toward him. "Then tell me what happened."

"Two men entered my shop demanding protection money…"

There was an uproar from outside and I held my finger up one more time. "Give me a moment."

I stepped out the door with Serafine right behind me. The noise was coming from the alley and I stepped around the corner where a crowd of people were staring at something on the wall.

I pushed through the crowd. "Looks like the Prince has everything well in hand."

Serafine snorted.

"What?" I glanced back at her.

"Really?"

I shrugged and retrieved the sack that was nailed to the wall right under two severed hands. I turned to walk away.

"You're just gonna leave those?"

"Those were warning. This, I would

wager, is the extortion money they took from the Baker."

"True. But those are going to start smelling soon."

"I don't buy bread here."

"He didn't have any sticky buns," she said with a shrug.

I met the Baker on the porch and pitched him the sack. "Looks like your problem is solved already. The Prince backs up what you paid him with action. You might want to do something with the warning on your wall in the alley, though."

"Where was this theft we were going to look into?" Serafine said as we step back into the street.

"A little further south."

She was looking at me with narrowed eyes.

"What?"

"I was just trying to figure if it was possible that you were the Prince."

"Me?"

"This unholy obsession with hands…"

"It was only the one time."

"Here." She stepped past me and proceeded south.

CHAPTER THIRTEEN

"You know there's no way I could be the Prince."

"How do you figure?"

"Do you honestly think I would be out here working?" I asked. "If I brought in the gold that he does, I sure as hell wouldn't be out here walking the street."

"True enough," she said. "You'd be shacked up with your Fallanasi girl."

"There's nothing wrong with Alicia."

"I never said there was. The fact that you've been back a second time speaks volumes for the girl. Could be she's special, could just be she's talented. But one thing's for certain, this is the first time I've ever seen you return."

"Hmpf."

"Just saying."

"There's the shop." I pointed toward a weapon shop.

"That's okay, change the subject."

"Don't know what you're talking about," I said and walked toward the weapon shop.

"Of course you don't."

There was a pretty good array of weapons lined up along the front of the store. I didn't see anyone standing near them but a medium-sized young man stepped out the door as I approached.

"Welcome!" He was about to enter his salesman spiel.

"Not here to shop," I said. "Looking for a Silas Nor."

"That's my boss," the man said. "I'm Tallison. Anything you have to say to him can be said to me."

"Well, I need to talk to your boss, Tallison."

"I said you can tell me."

"I heard you."

"Then what is the problem?" He was turning a little red.

"This is Marine business." My hand rested on the sword at my hip. "Where is Silas Nor?"

"He's inside, but—"

"Step aside while you're still able." My voice was cold.

Then he saw Serafine and his breath caught.

He wanted to say more but he thought better of it and stepped to the right.

I walked past the salesman. I've always been a pretty good judge of character and I could generally go on a first impression. My first impression of Tallison wasn't a very good one. Something was just…off.

After he saw Serafine there was something in his eyes that wasn't there before. It wasn't fear which was a common thing around her. There was something in his eyes that I didn't like one bit and I wasn't sure exactly what it was.

I waited at the door till Serafine stepped in and then I followed her. Tallison started to follow us and I shut the door in his face.

"That was a little rude," Serafine said.

"He can stay outside," I responded.

At least he could take a hint. He didn't try to enter again.

Across the room sitting at a table was an older man. You could look at him and tell he used to be a very large person. Age had taken its toll on the man and muscles that had used a bulge were still present but he was leaner than I expect he used to be.

"I'm guessing you're Silas," I said as I approached.

"I am."

"We're here about a report of stolen weapons."

He nodded and motioned toward the bench across from him at the table. "They must have taken my report very seriously to send you two."

"Marines take every case seriously, sir." Serafine said as she sat down across from him. "We would like to hear about the theft from you rather than read notes in a folder."

"I wouldn't think the theft of twelve swords would warrant sending the Marines who took down Redmane and his pet necromancer."

"It's just part of the job, sir," she said. "We investigate many crimes and we follow them wherever they lead. The case you mentioned started with a burglary."

"Well let's hope this theft doesn't do anything similar." He grinned. "Honestly, I think I know where they went but I have no proof."

"Your man out front have anything to do with it?" I asked.

"Funny you should say that," he answered.

"Perhaps you should let him in," Serafine said looking over her shoulder at me.

I shrugged and returned to the door to

open it. Looking out onto the porch there was no sign of Tallison.

"Innocent people don't run," I said as I turned back around. "I think your boy, Tallison, has chosen the better part of valor."

Silas sighed. "There was so much promise in that kid. Something changed a few weeks ago. I have no idea what it is but he wasn't the same kid he used to be. I hated even thinking that he was behind it, but everything pointed toward Tallison taking the swords."

"You're probably right," Serafine said. "We'll put a warrant out for him. When we pick him up I'll get to the truth."

"Thanks for coming out," he said, his shoulders sagging. "I don't know what I'm going to do, now."

"I know a kid down in the Commons," I said. "He's a pretty good kid and I don't think he would say no if someone offered to teach him a profession that might actually get him out of the Commons."

"Most of the kids down there get pulled into the gangs."

"He's managed to stay out of them so far. If you're interested, I'll get him up here to see you."

"It's hard work and I don't coddle anyone."

"That's what the kid needs, Silas."

"Then send the boy up and I'll talk to him. I'm not making any promises here, but I'll give him a fair shake."

"That's all I ask. Maybe it'll be good for both of you."

He nodded.

"His name is Broadus. I don't think you'll be disappointed."

As I turned to head toward the door, Serafine was trying to hide a smile.

"What?"

"Nothing."

We stepped out on the porch and there was still no sign of Tallison.

"I guess we should get back to the station and fill out this warrant. We can find out if we have a sketch artist here in Sable. If not, we can run out to our old station and hit up Faile."

"We won't need to."

"Eh?"

"I saw him. I can create a likeness."

"Well that'll be handy," I said. "Why do we even bother with sketch artists?"

"Well I don't see everyone who commits a crime. We're just lucky enough to have seen this guy."

"Wait a minute. Didn't you see that guy about six months ago? I sat with that sketch artist for six hours."

"It was your fault he got away."

"What's that got to do with it?"

She shrugged and walked back toward our station laughing.

"Really? Was that a giggle?" I followed with my gaze roving across the crowds. "Asshole."

CHAPTER FOURTEEN

"You left something," Alicia said, holding up the talisman.

"Thought you might like to use it for the bath."

"I wondered if you would come back for it."

I stepped closer to her and wrapped my arms around her waist. "I didn't come back for the talisman."

"Also not what I expected from a Sword."

"I'll return until you tell me not to," I said. "Do you wish me to stop?"

She stepped back with a crooked smile and unclasped the dress to let it fall to the floor. "Not today, maybe I'll want you to stop tomorrow."

I grinned and swept her into my arms. "Then we'll just have to see what tomorrow brings."

SERAFINE WAITED ON THE FRONT PORCH IF Boggan's when I stepped out the door.

"Three days in a row?"

I shrugged. "I like her."

She smiled and walked into the street toward Sable. "Perhaps I should open a door so we don't eat a dozen sticky buns."

"We?"

"Of course." She pointed at me with a thumb. "You ate five of those we got yesterday. You won't be able to even swing a sword if you keep doing that."

"I ate five? You sure about that?"

"Certainly."

I shook my head and looked up at the overcast sky. "Reckon it'll rain?"

She uttered a word of power and stopped for a second.

"In about a half an hour."

"I'm pretty sure that's cheating."

"You're the one who asked." She shrugged and continued walking.

When we stepped into Merrick, I admit, I was a little disappointed when the smell of fresh sticky buns was absent.

The baker's door was closed, even though I could see some movement behind the rippled glass. I could hear curses from inside through the broken pane in the lower left corner of the window. It was a common sight in the Merrick District. Shopkeepers in Merrick were successful enough to have glass panes but they were expensive. Replacing one might take a long time.

Most of the shops in the Parch District didn't have glass at all and nowhere in Sable would have any with all of the violence. Fights tended to be hard on expensive glass.

I stepped up to the door and opened it to find a younger version of the man we met carrying a pan toward a table on the left side of the display room. The smell of fresh bread assailed my nostrils.

"Can I help you?" he asked. "I'm getting a late start today so I have limited stock this morning. I can't believe my father just walked out."

"Walked out?" I asked.

"He just quit the business and left. Told me he was done."

"I met your father yesterday. He seemed pretty happy. He was going to order me some naranga honey."

"I can still do that, but I have to dig into his ledgers to get the name of his contact."

"It's not a rush. You look pretty busy. I'll stop by in a few days and we'll do that." I turned to leave but paused. "Did he give any sort of reason? Was someone hassling him or anything? If it's something the Marines can help with…"

"He didn't say." The baker shrugged. "He came in real late last night. I feel like something happened but I have no idea what it was."

"No injuries?"

"He seemed perfectly healthy. This morning he looked around and said he was through. Then walked out the door and down the street towards Parch."

I nodded and stepped back out the door.

"That seemed odd," Serafine said.

"It did."

"Should we go to the Merrick station and see if someone will look into it?"

I looked back at the bakery. "What can we really tell them? Ask them to investigate someone that decided to quit his job? It feels off but I doubt they'll look into it if they have a typical caseload."

"True." She walked toward Parth. "It just seems odd to me and something feels wrong about it. Not just normal wrong."

"Magic wrong?"

"Maybe."

"That's not what I want to hear. Sorcerous involvement is always worse."

"Really?"

"You weren't the one who got set on fire."

"It was just the one time."

"Does it need to be more than once? I don't think anyone needs to be set on fire twice."

"Some people need to be set on fire multiple times. Maybe not you, but some people need it. Remember that guy we brought in for abusing his daughters?"

"Yeah, he needs to be set on fire on a regular basis." I nodded. "Although getting stuck in prison is suitable too. Many of the inmates have children of their own. They have little use for a guy who hurts kids. I hear he's having a pleasant time in the Tombs."

The Tombs was the prison located on an island just off the coast. You could just see it from the harbor. Prisoners were shipped out to the Tombs and occasionally someone would be brought back from the Tombs after serving their time.

"Maybe Redmane set him on fire out there."

"Not without hands. Hard to do ritualist magic without hands."

"True enough. Maybe someone else did it."

"You really have a thing about someone getting set on fire?"

"Well I missed it when you did it that one time. I was busy."

"I don't intend to have a repeat, so you're just gonna have to live without that particular experience."

"I suppose. But who knows? I might get lucky."

Sure enough, about a half an hour after I'd asked the large droplets began to hit the cobblestones.

Serafine uttered a word of power and the rain hit a glowing shield over her head.

"That's okay, I don't need a rain shieldy thing," I grumbled.

"What?"

"Nothing." I raised the hood on my cloak.

CHAPTER FIFTEEN

"Two cases solved in as many days," Donavan said. "Any leads on the murder?"

"Not yet," Serafine answered. "We're going back to talk to Cobb today. Possibly do some canvasing of the area around where she was found on the way over. Many people won't admit when they saw something."

I held up the truth talisman I'd checked out of the armory. "This should take care of that."

"Talismans," she muttered.

"It would be pretty obvious if you cast spells every time we talk to someone."

"Doesn't mean I like them."

"Of course you don't. I wonder if they have any of those rain thingies in a talisman."

"Would you like a rain shield? All you had to do is say so." She stepped out of the Sergeant's office.

Donovan laughed at the scowl on my face. Then he pulled another folder from the drawer.

"Here's another one."

"Another murder?"

"Almost. She was found early enough to get the Medics to her. Seems the guy who found her was carrying a talisman that stabilized her until the Medic arrived."

"Lucky."

"Not as sure of that as you are. She was torn up pretty bad."

"The Priestess should be able to get rid of most of it," I said.

"She is a Priestess of Shalira. It's hard to get Shalira to take a hand in the matter when the girl is a worshiper of Madrigal."

"That might be difficult."

"The Medics can heal her but without Divine help, she'll carry the scars."

"Damn. I was lucky Shalira didn't have conflicts with the Three. Carrying the memories is bad enough but the scars would have been a lot worse. What about a Priest of Madrigal?"

"A runner has been sent."

"Where's the girl?"

"In the trauma center at the Noskomeon."

"Serafine will definitely want to go see

her. Maybe we can get a description of this prick."

The Noskomeon was back down toward Temple Row. If my recent study of Rhymen history served me, the Noskomeon was built after the Empire conquered Daramacles. Rhyme was always willing to take anything they could use and the Medics were very good at healing. They used sorcery of all types but were known more for thaumaturges and talismanics than ritualists or evokers. Ritualists were rare and evokers rarer still.

If the Medics couldn't heal someone, they were in a pretty bad way. Like when a fire sorcerer sets a person on fire.

I owed Shalira for that. I was fairly certain the Three didn't have issue with Shalira for healing me. My connection to my gods was still intact. If I had been conscious at the time, perhaps things may have been different.

"Not a pleasant day for being out on the streets," Donavan said.

"We don't really get a choice do we?"

He chuckled. "Not much of one. You can walk in the rain or through one of those doors your partner makes."

"Don't say that too loudly. She'll hear you and want to use the doors."

"I've heard stories of people lost traveling through doors like that."

"Thank the gods you can't attach that spell to a talisman."

"That one is just done by ritualists or evokers."

I turned to follow Serafine. "What bothers me is that I even know that. In Fallanasi, sorcerers are rare. Here, it seems like you trip over one every time you step outside."

"Rhyme has always been a safe haven for sorcerers where many places they are persecuted."

I shrugged. "Fallanasi would have accepted a sorcerer if the majority of the ones who showed up didn't try to destroy the country."

"No offense intended, I'm not talking about Fallanasi in particular. The Redulans execute any sorcerer they find in their country. Fyraxxi are just as bad."

"No offense taken, Sarge."

"Then there're places like Dum." He grimaced.

"Black Sorcerers," I said. "I reckon they have to be bad when they name their country Doom."

Donavan chuckled as I exited.

Serafine was at her desk and I set the folder in front of her. "We got another victim. This one survived, though."

"Oh?"

"She's at the Noskomeon."

"The Medics? Not Dianna?"

"Shalira won't heal a worshiper of Madrigal."

"Damn."

"Yep. Wanna go interview her?"

She stood up with the folder in her hand. "Absolutely. I'll open a door so you don't get your precious hair wet."

"You could just make me a rain shield."

"Where's the fun in that?"

She said a word of power and the portal appeared right in front of us. Simms jerked as the portal appeared right beside his desk.

"Grisham's gnarly ghost, woman! Give a little warning, won't you?"

"Much more fun this way," she said with a grin and stepped into the opening.

I sighed and followed her into the dark.

"Stupid doors," I muttered.

"What?" she asked.

"Nothing."

The glowing portal on the other end of the dark tunnel seemed about twice as far as the last time. My eye was twitching by the time we reached it.

"You did that on purpose, didn't you?" I asked as I stepped out of the portal into a deluge of rain. Water flooded off of her rain shield into my face. "Asshole."

"I don't know what you're talking about." She stepped forward under the portico of the Noskomeon. "Did you get your hair wet?"

"Not sure why I even bother," I muttered and stepped into the dry. "You couldn't have put the damned opening under the overhang?"

She shrugged and grinned. "I suppose I could have."

"Asshole."

She chuckled and strode through the door.

A robed man met us in the foyer eyeing our Marine tabards. "You are here to see the girl?"

"If she's up to it," Serafine responded. "I'd like to find this guy before he does it again."

"No doubt. The Priest of Madrigal is with her at the moment."

I could hear the disdain in his voice. Madrigal is a hard sell to many, including myself.

"We'll wait until he's done."

The Medic nodded and motioned for us to follow.

After a few moments and a short maze of hallways we stood outside of a curtained opening. I could hear sobbing inside.

The curtain opened and a rail thin pale fellow stepped out.

"Madrigal healed the girl?" I asked.

"Our Lord of Unbridled Delight will not

sacrifice the pleasure of one for the pleasure of another."

"Because this prick took pleasure in cutting the girl up?" I asked.

"Indeed."

I grimaced. "Wouldn't the pleasure be compounded if he received his pleasure from the act and the girl received her pleasure from the healing?"

The priest scowled. "Who are you to question the decisions of my Lord?"

His boney finger prodded my chest.

"I'm the guy that will remove the offending appendage if you poke me again." I looked down at his hand. "And I'll take great pleasure in it."

The priest withdrew his finger.

"If you're not gonna help the girl, you'd best remove yourself from my presence, priest. You can tell your Lord I'm going to find this bastard and I'm gonna really enjoy cutting his damn head off."

I stepped forward and shouldered past the useless priest.

"You touch that dagger and he won't have to worry about cutting off appendages," Serafine said.

I turned just as she dropped her hood and stared directly into the priest's eyes where he could see exactly what she was. He gasped and took his empty hand from the slit in the side of his robe and hurried down the hallway.

"I take it neither of you are very fond of the followers of Madrigal?" the Medic asked with a small grin.

"Not so much," I said. "Some of their actions are questionable, to say the least. Madrigal doesn't seem to differentiate the various ways his followers enjoy pleasure. Some people gain pleasure from some pretty awful things."

"Agreed," he responded.

"Sylvyne has no use for their ilk," Serafine said as she walked past me to stand next to the girl lying in the bed sobbing.

A nurse was applying new bandages to her wounds.

"A God who would leave one of his followers like this is not a God I would follow," muttered the nurse.

I couldn't help but agree in this case. Some gods do not specialize in healing like Shalira, but they are still capable of doing so. The ways the gods healed their followers varied with the particular god and some of them might even be worse than the injuries they heal. I didn't know what version of healing Madrigal would use but his refusal to heal one of his own only increased my dislike.

The girl's wounds looked like they were

days old even though she had arrived at the Noskomeon last night. The medics were very talented and the potions they used were some of the best. The guy who did this had really done a number on her though. I could see well over a dozen cuts just in the upper half of her body.

"Did you see who did this to you?" Serafine asked.

The girl nodded.

"Just think about him for a moment, picture him in your mind."

The girl's eyes widened as a word of power rolled through the room.

"There he is," Serafine said with her eyes glowing green.

"He is protected by my Lord."

"Then perhaps your Lord will be interested in how much pleasure I will take in sending this dog to meet him." Serafine stood. She turned to me. "That's all I need."

"All right then." I touch the hilt of one of my swords. "Let's go get this prick."

CHAPTER SIXTEEN

I slung the leather strap over my shoulder and let the document bag hang under my left arm as we walked out of our headquarters.

"I still can't believe you left me with that sketch artist for six hours. You never even told me you could do something like that."

Serafine shrugged. "You never asked."

"Why would I think to ask if you could make magic pictures?"

"The Sergeant asked."

"So?"

"He seemed to be aware that some sorcerers can do this."

"And where was I supposed to find that out? You're the only sorcerer I know."

"Then perhaps you should have asked."

"Asshole."

She chuckled. "Want me to make a door?"

"Hells no."

"It would be a lot faster." She raised a hand.

"We have to spread these flyers."

"Hmph."

"If you're going to be eating sticky buns by the dozen, you need to walk anyway."

"Are you saying I'm fat?"

"I would never say anything like that," I said. "Maybe a little pudgy, but never fat."

"I am *not* pudgy."

"Whatever you say." I grinned.

"He really does have a death wish," Sergeant Donovan said as he stepped up behind us.

"Don't know what you're talking about, boss," I said.

"That's why you're working in Sable District."

"He might have a point," Serafine said. "It's also the reason *I'm* working in Sable District. I told Major Alan it was a bad idea."

"What was a bad idea?"

"Partnering me with an idiot."

"I feel like I should be offended," I said. "Should I be offended, boss?"

"The truth is a painful thing, son."

"I'll take that as a yes."

"Have you heard anything else about the missing bodies?" he asked.

"Not yet, we're planning to go to the

Market District and talk to Cobb again. He should have gone to see Meere by now."

"Let me know what you find out."

"Will do," I said.

Donovan nodded and returned to the station.

I glanced back at Donovan with a grin and turned to follow Serafine into the busy street.

"It's strange we haven't gotten any messenger from Cobb," I said. "Seemed like he was planning on going straight to see Meere."

"It does seem odd," she responded. "Cobb seemed fairly competent."

"I thought you had a problem with him, considering the relationship he had with the pleasure girl."

"I had some time to think about what you said. You actually might be right."

"Did you just say I might be right?"

"I've told you it happens rarely enough. I feel like it should be acknowledged when it happens."

"I'll take it."

She chuckled.

Reaching the market district didn't take that long when there wasn't some sort of distraction along the way. Rogue sorcerers, knife fights, attempted assassinations, and such.

Cobb was working the front desk when we stepped into the Marine post.

He looked at us with his head cocked to the side a bit. "Wasn't really expecting you. Not much I can tell you that I didn't include in the message."

"Message?" I asked.

"Messenger was sent yesterday."

"We didn't get anything."

"That's weird. Our messenger service is typically pretty good." He picked up a form and looked at it. "Yep, says Dever should have been there yesterday."

"Since we didn't get any message, we decided to come talk to you ourselves. What did you find out?"

"Meere is definitely alive."

He sounded uncertain.

"Seems like there's another shoe yet to drop," Serafine said.

"I swear it's her but it just doesn't seem like her. I don't even know how to explain it. It's like she's a totally different person now."

"That doesn't sound good at all," she said.

"I know sorcery can do a lot of things," he said. "But can it replace a person with another?"

"Did she not know you?"

"She knew me. But there's something

missing. I swear I don't know how to explain it."

"Definitely strange," I said. "But she's definitely alive, correct?"

"Definitely."

"We have to run down to the Commons. You'll keep an eye on her?" Serafine asked.

"I will. I feel like something bad is happening."

"You're not the only one," she said. "Something bad, something big. I can feel it."

We turned and stepped back out of the Marine post.

"We need to go see this Meere," Serafine said.

"Why?"

"If my suspicions are correct, I might be able to see what's wrong."

"As in see with sorcery?"

"Yes."

"What are your suspicions?"

"I don't even want to speak them aloud yet," she said. "Not until I've seen her."

"Then we should go now."

She nodded and we turned left toward the pleasure house instead of right toward the Commons.

We stepped inside to find the same Madam lounging in a chair.

"Business again?"

"We're here to see Meere."

"I don't know what's gotten into that woman. She left here this morning and I haven't seen her since. On top of that I'm missing some jewelry."

"You think she might have stolen it?" I asked.

"I never would've thought that of her, but lately, she's been acting really strange."

"Send a runner to the Marine post and informed Marine Cobb. We'll get an investigation started." Serafine turned around and walked back out of the pleasure house.

"She ran?" I asked.

"If my suspicion is right, she did. I doubt if she'll ever return here."

"So what's you're suspicion?"

"Necromancy."

"Shit."

CHAPTER SEVENTEEN

"He seemed like a decent sort," I said. "More importantly, it's an opportunity for you to get out of here."

"What about mom?" The husky young man asked.

"Apprenticeship to a blacksmith would be a good way to get your mother out of here, too. You probably couldn't get her out of here immediately but a little ways down the road it would be a possibility."

"I'll go see him."

"Good," I said as Serafine and I returned to the street leaving Broadus standing on the small stoop. "I'd love to see you away from all this."

I saw Vienna, Broadus's mother, watching from a window. She smiled and waved.

"Not a coincidence that his mother is quite pretty?" Serafine asked.

"I don't know what you're talking about."
She snorted.

"What?"

"Nothing." She grinned.

Bells began to clamor across the city.

"Shit," I cursed under my breath.

"I couldn't have said it better," she said. "Donovan said there was a fleet coming in today."

The bells clamored when Rhymen naval vessels pulled into port.

"Gonna be a rough time with that many sailors on leave."

"That's all we need with a possible necromancer loose in the city." She frowned. "Best we get back to Sable District."

I looked back one more time at Vienna. I knew she would be happy to see her son get out of the Commons.

"She was quite pretty," Serafine said. "Did you ever think of returning with that one?"

I chuckled. "You're not gonna let that go are you?"

"Nope."

"Fine. Yes I met her soon after coming to Rhyme. I've never thought about going back to anyone until now. Would I have thought about it if it happened now? Who knows?"

We almost made it back to Sable before the first sailors hit the port. We almost reached the Marine post before we ran into the first fight.

"Every time…" Serafine cursed.

"I got this one," I said and waded into the crowd of sailors surrounding the two struggling individuals.

One of the individuals wore the tabard of a Marine. Sailors and Marines were like oil and water. They were never going to get along.

"He's got backup!" The voice came from the left end of the crowd.

A large sailor stepped into my path. He was close to seven feet tall.

A loud whistle came from my right and the sailor stiffened.

"Porter! Do you remember what happened at the last port?"

"Aye, Sir!"

"Look at the man before you. Do you see something you might recognize?"

His eyes looked down and rested on the two swords at my sides.

"Fallanasi?"

I nodded.

"My apologies."

The fight had ended as they watched the exchange. The sailor who had been fighting the Marine eased back into the crowd.

Porter nodded and rejoined the crowd himself.

The officer had blown the whistle stepped forward. "These dumb asses pick a fight every time they step off the boat. I should've let you hand him his ass."

"He looked like he would be a handful." I nodded toward the big man who was a foot taller than anyone else in the crowd.

"He's a handful all right. We saw a couple of guys tangle with a Fallanasi Sword at our last port. None of these guys want any of that. It was the damnedest thing I've ever seen. He took those boys apart before they could even touch him. I'm right, aren't I? You're a Sword?"

"I used to be. I'm just a Marine now."

"Sure you are," he said with a grin. "We'll try to keep it as civil as we can while we're in port. There's no way I can keep it all under control just promise me you won't kill any of them."

"I'll do my best. You tell your boys to keep the blades in their scabbards and we'll do just fine."

"That's all I can ask and I'll relay the word."

"That was interesting," Serafine said as the officer rejoined his sailors. "I'm beginning to think a Sword is a little bit more than just a Marine. I'm guessing you weren't just city guards."

I shrugged.

"All right, keep your secrets. Let's get to the shop so the boss can give out the assignments."

I nodded and followed her, touching my lips, chest, and right arm in turn.

"Sword of the Fallanasi, chosen of the Three…"

CHAPTER EIGHTEEN

"Crimes have been at a record low this time," Donovan said, looking at a room full of confused Marines. "I'm not sure what happened but I'll take it. Three hundred and eighty-two sailors over three days and there were only seven fights that needed to be interrupted. I'm impressed."

"I wonder what happened," Serafine muttered beside me. "I'm even more convinced of what I said a few days ago."

I shrugged.

"One day you're going to have to tell me exactly what it means to be a Sword of the Fallanasi. I've heard the term used more in the last three days than in the whole year before."

"It's not really something we talk about."

"I got very curious about it yesterday."

"That doesn't bode well," I said.

"Why?"

"When you get curious about something, you tend to dig until you're not curious anymore."

"That's not really a bad thing," she said.

"Not bad for an investigator."

"Are you trying to ask me not to pry?"

I shrugged again.

"Your friend, Alicia, wouldn't say much and there was surprisingly little in the House of Knowledge about Fallanasi so what I learn will be at your discretion. I won't push if you don't want to talk about it."

"Swords didn't apply for the job. Swords were chosen and sworn to the Archon."

"So the Archon chose those with talent."

"Something like that."

We weren't chosen by the Archon. We were chosen by the Three, but most people didn't really understand that part. It's not something we ever talked about as Swords. When dealing with gods there is always a price. When the priest of Shalira healed me, she took every one of those wounds upon herself before Shalira healed them. She felt every one of them. Dealing with gods always has a price.

Before I could say any more, two sailors stepped into the room and moved to the sides of the door. They were followed by an officer.

"Admiral?" Donovan asked.

"Sergeant."

"What can we do for you sir?"

"I came to file a report, Sergeant."

"And I was just telling the men that I was impressed at the lack of problems."

"The men do get a little rambunctious when they come ashore but they always come back to the ship. It's not uncommon to lose one or two men during shore leave but we're missing thirty-four men."

"Thirty-four? What the hell?"

"It's an unusually high number." The admiral stepped forward. "Like I said, it's common to lose one or two."

"I'll put everyone on it, sir."

"Thank you Sergeant. I'll delay departure for another day but I'll keep the men on the ships."

"I'll send a couple of the investigators with you to get a list of names." He turned toward us. "Kort and Serafine will escort you back and return with a list."

The admiral nodded, replaced the hat upon his head, and turned to us.

"Right behind you, sir."

He nodded to me in response and walked out the door followed by his two sailors, Serafine, and me.

He didn't speak as we followed him through the crowds toward the docks.

"This doesn't look good," I muttered just loud enough for Serafine to hear. "Watch the crowd."

"There's something wrong," she said louder.

"Excuse me?" The admiral asked coming to a halt.

"On your guard, men," he said as he eyed the crowd that had grown in size.

"How far to the ship?" I asked. The direction we were going was suddenly full of people too. "Never mind that."

A man stepped forward from the crowd. "Give us the admiral and you can walk away."

My eye was twitching and my hands rested on the hilts of my swords. "Counter offer. You walk away and I'll leave you the use of your legs."

"You're in no place to bargain, Marine. Give us the admiral."

"Move to your left, sir. Back to the wall. You two, guard him."

"That's an awful lot of men, Marine. What are you going to do?" The admiral asked.

My swords were in my hands in the blink of an eye. "I reckon we'll kill them."

I heard blades drawn behind me. "Five against that crowd is better than two."

The original speaker stepped back and

motioned to those around the small group. "Kill them."

"There is a darkness intertwined with their souls," Serafine whispered. "Necromancy."

She stepped forward toward the crowd. "You have no idea what you're facing."

"You are the one who has no idea what they're facing. We are the undying." The original speaker stayed close to the back as the others began to close in.

"This is true death, thrall. There will be no coming back."

"Kill them all," he said.

"So be it!" Serafine took another step forward and a word of power echoed through the square.

She glanced back toward me with smoldering eyes.

"I have your back," I said.

A word of power boomed across the square as the crowd charged toward us to be met with a wall of flame. Another word and an explosion sent bodies flying in every direction. And yet another produced a torrent of flame from her right hand. I remembered Redmane when he was using his fire magic. There was nothing he did that was anything like the power levels Serafine used. Word after word boomed across the square. Men were consumed in ice and hit with spikes of earth from the ground sending shattered pieces in all directions. Then the flames were pushed with gusts of wind to spread to them as well. Sable Square became a pyre. Serafine's eyes glowed white as all the color combined when she used all four elements.

She staggered and I stepped in to support her. More words of power boomed across the square. I could feel every one of them shake her as I held an arm to support her. The flames finally dwindled and Serafine slumped. My breath caught as I eased her to the ground looking for a wound.

"I'm fine," she said softly. "Takes a lot out of you. Just need to rest…"

I looked back up to see the only surviving member of the attackers was the original speaker. He turned to run and I stood up, drew a small knife, and threw it. The man stumbled and fell on his face.

He tried to get up but his legs wouldn't function. The knife had severed his spine.

"Grisham's ghost!" The admiral stepped forward looking at the devastated crowd. All that was left of close to a hundred people was ash and bone. He looked into her multicolored eyes. "Many who can use all of the branches of sorcery can barely touch each. You, milady, are wasted as a Marine."

CHAPTER NINETEEN

"What the devil happened?" Donovan asked as I helped Serafine through the door.

"There was an ambush," I said as she eased into the chair behind her desk. "They were after the admiral. It's official, necromancy sucks."

"Necromancy?"

"Yeah. Ninety-five or a hundred of them came at us."

"Necromancers?" His voice was a couple octaves higher.

"No. Thralls."

"Gods!"

"She made sure they wouldn't be coming back." I motioned toward Serafine whose head was drooping. "She needs a bed in the barracks tonight. She used a lot of power today. Not to mention the square will never be the same."

"They attacked in the square?"

"Right out in the middle of it. There's a lot of cleanup needed. Redmane had nothing on her. She roasted the lot of them. I knew she was powerful but…" I let the sentence trail off as I caught Serafine when she slipped from the chair.

I lifted her in my arms and carried her toward the barracks. She was so light I almost couldn't even believe she was the same titan that had ripped the earth asunder in Sable Square.

She smiled drowsily as I placed her in one of the bunks. She mumbled something I didn't quite catch and was out.

Pulling the fur blanket up and over her, I stared at her sleeping face for a moment, brushed the white hair from in front of her eyes, and stood at attention mere feet in front of her sleeping form. My hands rested on the hilts of my swords as I stood guard.

"She's safe here," Donavon said. "You can go if you want. We'll keep a guard."

"I'm fine right here."

He nodded. "If you need anything, we're here."

"The list of names is still needed from the admiral. Can you send someone to the docks?"

"Absolutely."

"Thanks, boss."

"They might want to bypass the square. It's a mess."

I STEPPED OUT INTO THE BULLPEN TO FIND Simms crossing the room with a familiar brown bag.

"Sticky buns? Did the baker show back up?"

"His son made them. I heard they were her favorite and convinced him to make a batch."

"She'll appreciate them."

"I saw the square as I went for the list. Haven't seen anything like that since the war."

"Lakoshis?"

He nodded. "Used to work with a mixed unit of sorcerers and infantry. Called one of their squads a mage squad. Four sorcerers, one of each branch."

"I've heard of them."

"That's what Sable Square looks like. Like a mage squad was there. She did that by herself?"

"She did."

"Gods," he said with a shake of his head. "I've never seen one person with all the branches able to use them at those sort of levels."

"It was impressive."

"Give her these when she wakes. We got a hit on the killer you guys were after. Me and Jace are going to check out the lead."

"We'll be joining you as quick as we can. Just leave us directions to where you're going. I'll wake her and see if she's recovered."

I took the bag of sticky buns and returned to the barracks. I was still a couple of feet from her bunk when her eyes opened.

"Is that what I think it is?"

"More than likely. Simms convinced the Baker's son to whip up a batch of them this morning."

"Oh my." She pushed the furs aside and sat up. "I'm famished."

"I didn't take any of them. Figured you'd be hungry this morning."

"I could probably spare one," she said as she opened the bag. "Maybe."

She sniffed. "Why do you still smell like a firepit?"

"He's been standing guard all night," Donovan said from the door.

"Why? We're in a guard barracks."

I ate my sticky bun.

"Fine."

"Maybe it's not me that smells like a firepit," I said.

"Hmpf."

"Just sayin'…"

"You're not implying that I smell, are you."

"Of course not… stinky."

"Son," Donovan said. "I just got back from the square and I'm convinced you have a death wish when you say things like that."

"I don't know what you're talking about." I turned back to Serafine. "Simms said they got a lead on our killer and they went to check it out. You wanna join them or are you going to sleep all day?"

"Really?" she scrambled from the bunk. "You should have led with that."

I handed her the parchment with the location.

"That can't be right," she said. "I know this place."

"It's in the high district," I said.

"I know." She started for the door and swayed a little. "Damn. Still a little weak from yesterday."

"Perhaps we should leave it to Simms and Jace."

"I can't do that. I know who lives there."

"What?"

"Marcus Pel. I grew up with him. It can't be him."

"You saw the face the girl identified. Is it this Marcus fellow?" I asked.

"I haven't seen him in years."

"Maybe we should go see. Sure you're up to it?"

She said a word of power and took a deep breath. "It's temporary at best, but I'll be fine."

You could almost see the vitality build in her from the spell and she strode out of the outpost with me following.

CHAPTER TWENTY

As we passed Boggan's Tavern, I wondered how Alicia was doing. I hadn't been back in a few days because of all that was going on. I had sent a messenger to let her know what was happening so she didn't think I had chosen just to disappear. It was an odd thing for a Sword to do but it felt right.

Serafine staggered a moment as her spell was beginning to wear off. I stepped forward where she could lean on my shoulder.

"It's not much further," she said. "It can't be Marcus."

It sounded like she was trying to convince herself more than she was trying to convince me.

"How long has it been?"

"I knew him before my sorcery came to me. Fourteen years."

"Person can change a lot in fourteen years."

"But Madrigal? And to do what was done to those girls? Could he have changed that much?"

"He was someone you cared for."

"He was my first love."

Something connected in my mind as we rounded the corner. The girl at the Noskomeon might have been a sister if I had been looking at them standing together. If Serafine had dark hair instead of white they might've been twins.

"He's the one," I said remembering how Cobb had looked at Serafine when he first met us.

I would wager Meere would look a lot like Serafine as well. As would Lorette.

"How can you suddenly be so certain?" She asked as we rounded the corner a half a block from our destination.

Metal clashed ahead of us in the midst of a small crowd directly in front of the house we were looking for.

I couldn't see much through the crowd but Serafine said a word of power and the crowd was pushed aside as we approached.

Simms was facing a tall well-dressed man who wielded two swords. The crumpled form of the other Marine was off to the left and

Simms was holding his arm while trying to keep his axe raised.

A swordsman who uses two swords at once is either very skilled or foolhardy. Judging by the crumpled form of a Marine and another wounded, my guess would be skilled.

Marcus paused as he saw the Marine tabards. Then his eyes met hers.

"You!"

Serafine shoulders slumped and she realized I was correct.

I stepped in front of her.

"Who are you?" He asked eyeing the pair of swords at my waist. "Fancy yourself a swordsman do you?"

"I'll deal with this, Simms," I said as I drew my swords and stepped past the injured axman.

"Who are you? I have never seen your kind."

"Pity you won't have a chance to meet any more of my kind."

"Hah!"

He lunged forward using a form I learned when I was twelve. I learned the counter the same year. I also learned the move that countered that as well as the next twenty or so in that sequence. We were only five steps into the maneuver when he stepped back.

"Impressive," he said as we circled.

"You have a single chance to survive this, Pel." I tilted my head toward Serafine. "I would prefer not to kill someone she cared for right in front of her, although you deserve much worse for what you did to those girls. Lay down your arms face the consequences and I will let you live."

"You will let me live? We have only begun to dance this dance, you black skinned devil!"

"You are refusing?"

"You are damned right."

He charged forward and I heard Serafine's intake of breath. I stepped aside with a deft flick of my right hand blade leaving a two inch cut on his right cheek.

"Then I suppose the punishment should fit the crime."

He touched his cheek and his hand came away bloody.

"How many wounds did the Medic say she had?"

"What?" He looked confused.

"I'm not talking to you," I said.

"Twenty-four," Serafine answered.

Her answer told me everything I needed to know. Her answer was her way of giving me her permission to do what needed to be done.

He charged me once again swords moving in an elegant form common to master swordsmen. The man was indeed skilled, but when that maneuver was finished he was bleeding from seven more cuts.

"Not so much fun from the other end, is it?"

"My Lord… help me…"

"Your Lord would not sacrifice the pleasure of one to please another. That is what the priest said when he would not heal the girl. Somehow I don't think he's listening."

Pel screamed and charged me again. Even in his madness he was a very good swordsman.

"As a swordsman, you were one of the best. But your master was just a man," I said as I delivered the twenty fourth cut.

He toppled forward onto his face.

Simms and Serafine were checking on Jace but he shook his head when I turned toward them.

Marines pushed the noisy crowd aside. Donovan stood beside Ellington, our former Sergeant.

"Kort." Ellington nodded toward me. I could hear the disdain in his voice. "How did I know it would involve you and her? Is that Marcus Pel?"

"It is."

"Would you care to enlighten me as to why Counselor Pel's son is lying there dying in the street?"

The raspy breathing from the wounded man ended.

"He's no longer dying, sir."

Ellington's left eye was twitching.

"He's been torturing and killing pleasure girls who look like her because he didn't have the balls to confront her. Three that we know of and probably more that we don't. He also killed a Marine when they attempted to arrest him. I would also wager that Counselor Pel knows what his son has been up to and has covered for him multiple times."

"He is still a counselor's son."

"Was."

"Report back to your Sergeant."

"Yes sir." I turned to Sergeant Donovan. "Reporting sir."

"Somewhere else."

"Right here is fine," Sergeant Donovan said.

"We found the killer, boss. He attacked."

"Thank you Detective."

I walked to Serafine who couldn't disguise the sadness from what had transpired.

"I'm sorry."

"You have nothing to be sorry for." She glanced toward the body. "He did this because of me."

"No. He did all this because of him."

"I left when my abilities began to surface."

"Went to be trained I would assume."

"Yes."

"None of this is on you." I nodded toward Pel. "People twist themselves up inside sometimes. And sometimes that end result isn't even recognizable as the person they were before."

She was quiet for a moment. "We should get Jace back to our post."

"Agreed."

I turned to Simms. "You need to get that arm checked out too."

CHAPTER TWENTY-ONE

"None of this is on you," I said as I followed Serafine, who was quieter than normal.

"He wasn't capable of this when I knew him. If only I'd—"

"What? Stayed with him and lost yourself when the magic overwhelmed you. I've seen where that leads. In Fallanasi there is no School of Sorcery. For most who learn of their powers, it is hidden as best they can and it drives many of them to madness. The ones with little ability do better than those with a strong affinity for one of the elements. When the madness comes, it is always the innocent that suffer."

"I know it in here," she pointed at her temple. Then at her heart, "But I feel different here."

"His madness was his own. He wasn't driven there by sorcery."

"How could I have been so wrong about him?"

"You were fourteen years old. How were you to judge what he would become?"

I caught movement from our right. A hooded figure was keeping pace with us. He was mostly hidden in the crowd, but I would catch a glimpse of him every so often. I saw him several times. I paid better attention to my left and, sure enough, there was another keeping pace. He wore the raiment of a noble but he moved like warrior. I recognized this because it was the way I moved through the city.

"Raise your shield."

"What?"

Regardless of the question, a word slipped through my mind and the shimmer appeared.

The "nobleman" smiled. He nodded to me and motioned for me to approach.

"Shadowing us is a good way to die," I said as I stopped about five feet from him. "This is not a good time."

"It's never a good time," he said.

Serafine stepped up behind me to the left.

"Beautiful and intelligent. She stays back, out of the way of your attack." He nodded toward her. "Greetings, Lady Serafine."

"Your man gets any closer and this will get real ugly real fast." I motioned back toward the crowd with my head. My hands remained very close to my swords.

He waved toward the crowd and the hooded figure slipped back into them.

"Darby is a little overprotective. Please forgive him."

"Alright," I said. "Let's get down to it then. What do you want? We've a dead Marine and another wounded that need attended to."

"Right to the point. I like that."

I nodded.

"I run an organization that has a contract with the Rhymen Marines. Part of my job is to inform them when something is wrong in Rhyme."

"The Prince."

"Yes."

"So what do you know about Necromancy?"

"Not much, which is still more than I would like to know. Is that where my people are disappearing to?"

"I would have thought you would know more than we do."

He grimaced. "Normally I would, but I've been out of the city for the last few months. Darby has been keeping tabs on things but he isn't an investigator. He knows something is wrong but he's more of a 'stab it til it stops being wrong' sort of person."

I chuckled. "I get that. I've worked with some of those types."

He shrugged. "What can you do? It's hard to find someone I trust enough with the right skill set to replace me."

"You're missing people?"

"Yes. All signs are that they just got sick of the life and walked away. I could see a couple in the last month, but sixty four?"

"I don't know what the turnover rate of criminals would be but sixty four does seem excessive."

"You don't approve of the deal I made with the Marines?"

"Understand? Yes. Approve? Who am I to say? I just work here."

"At least you're honest." He looked toward Serafine. "And you, Lady?"

"I remember the days before," she said. "Still doesn't mean I approve but I'm more partial to the deal than he is."

"I chose the right ones to approach. Most Marines give me the standard 'How can we help?' and promptly forget anything I say afterwards. I do prefer honesty. How do we know it's Necromancy?"

"We were attacked by close to a hundred

thralls yesterday who were after the Admiral of the fleet."

"The fact that you're here says they were unsuccessful."

"They were extremely unsuccessful."

"Perhaps I could see the bodies. I can identify my people if there were any."

"Not much way of identifying them," I said. "Not a great deal left after she introduced them to fire sorcery."

"That would make it a bit more difficult."

"Somewhere in this city someone is making thralls in great numbers." I motioned around us. "If you find where this is happening before we do, please inform us. If we find it, how do I send word to you?"

"Tell your Sergeant. They all know where to leave messages for me."

I nodded.

"Then I bid you farewell, Marine." He made a small bow. "Lady."

"Figured you were a noble," I said as he walked back the way he'd come.

"That's your take away from that conversation?"

"We already knew most of what he had to say."

"Sixty four of his people. Most of what I saw yesterday were dockworkers or commoners."

"Yeah. They didn't look much like the Prince's people. Of course he could have people in all walks of life." I started walking to catch up with the wagon where Jace was laying. "If it's bodies they need, then the Mortuary would be the place to start. What if we do some skulking tonight? You need to sleep some more, first, but we can follow the wagon to the mortuary tonight."

"That's a good idea," she said as her shield dropped.

She hid it well but she was still tired after the fight in the square.

"Then we get to the barracks and you sleep for a few hours. After that, we'll get to work."

"What about your girl, Alicia?"

"Already sent messages telling her we were in the middle of something big."

"You sent her a message." She was smiling.

"What?"

"You've never done that before either."

CHAPTER TWENTY-TWO

"Seem to be feeling better," I said.

"The nap and bath helped immensely. And the change of clothes." She plucked at the fabric. "Even if it's not quite my style."

"Part of a clothing shop robbery a few years back," Simms responded.

His arm was covered in a bandage although it didn't seem to be giving him any adverse effects. He'd refused to be left out of our evening endeavor.

"It is welcome considering the state of my clothes after the last two days."

"You two continue," I said. "I see someone and I'm going to check them out."

Dropping back, I crossed the street a good distance behind the figure I had spied.

"Hmpf," I grunted as I recognized the movements. "Darby. Okay, where's your boss?"

"Right here. Whoa!"

By the time he'd said the second word, I had spun around, drew a sword and held the tip to his throat.

"You're quiet, Prince."

"And you're fast. Never seen someone move like that. You ever consider another line of work?"

"Not likely. You shadowing us or the wagon?"

He grinned. "The wagon. I saw you a few moments ago. Then you dropped back. Figured you'd spied Darby. It seems we had the same thought."

"Figured if we wanted to find a Necromancer, we should follow the dead. You got any others out here?"

"Just Darby."

"We're three over there. Me, Serafine, and Simms. Probably a good thing for all of us to know so we don't bump heads."

"Agreed."

I dropped back once again and crossed the street.

"You have a nice conversation?" Serafine asked as I stepped up beside her again.

"As a matter fact I did. It seems the Prince had the same idea we had."

She tapped her ear where I noticed one of our listening talismans. "I heard."

"Thought you hated talismans."

"I do." She shrugged. "But they do have their uses."

Simms chuckled.

The wagon holding the bodies of Jace and three others that had turned up during the day entered the gates to the mortuary.

"Let's use that building to keep an eye on the wagon." She pointed at an abandoned building that looked as if it would collapse at any second.

As we slipped in the door, the Prince stepped from the shadows. "Hello again, my friends. Darby is watching the wagon."

"Prince." I nodded.

"I'll go join him," Simms said and headed in the direction the Prince had pointed.

The Prince smiled. "Such a lack of trust. Should I be offended?"

"Guess that's up to you."

"I suppose it wouldn't do any good anyway. I made a short trip over to the square and saw the cleanup efforts." He looked at Serafine. "You, milady, are quite terrifying. If the Marines ever choose to negate our pact, please give me a couple of hours to depart our fine city."

"The pact is in no danger, Prince." She kept looking in the direction Simms had gone.

"You are not used to delegating," he said.

"No, she's not."

"It's hard to do," he said. "And harder to find someone you can trust to delegate things to. Darby is one who would lay down his life before he would betray me."

I nodded. "Simms is a Marine."

"I do so love that about the Marines. It's why I came to your organization instead of the Royals. No offense intended, milady."

I glanced toward her. "Figured you for a noble. A Royal?"

"As far down the ranks of royalty as it's possible to be."

"Yet, you *are* a Royal." the Prince grinned.

"No more a Royal than you are," she said. "Not after I joined the Marines. Now I am a Marine."

I didn't miss his small reaction at her words. Perhaps he was more than a begger child who had made good.

"Believe what you wish, but Royals are forever Royals, milady."

"As much as I would prefer that to be false, I can't argue the point. My mother never lets me forget it."

"We have movement." Simms stepped from the darkness, axe in hand.

My eyes narrowed as I saw something drip from the blade.

"Shit."

He tensed. "Too observant for your own good."

He swung the huge blade at the Prince.

The Prince hadn't reached the top of his criminal empire by being slow. He rolled to the left and lost about an inch of his hair to the razor sharp axe.

A word of power echoed across the room and Simms was slammed backwards.

"You? A thrall?"

He shrugged and charged forward again.

Serafine uttered another word and he was engulfed in flame.

He stopped still as his body burned.

"You can't stop us this time. There are hundreds of us coming for you…"

His voice tapered off as the flames consumed him with not so much as a scream. He was staring at Serafine.

"This place is not defendable," I said, motioning toward the door. "We have to move, now."

Darby staggered into the light given off by the burning body. He had blood dripping from his cloak.

The Prince caught him as he toppled forward.

"Darby," he said in a soft voice. "I'm so sorry."

"Knew… it would… end this way. Foretold…"

He slumped.

"You came, anyway." He eased his friend to the floor. "You need to burn him. He wouldn't want that bastard to bring him back."

Serafine said the word again.

"We have to go!" I pointed toward the door. "They want her."

As we exited the door I could hear the stomp of many feet as they closed in from every direction.

"Shit."

Serafine said something but no sound came from her lips.

"Damn it all!"

I pointed back at the door. "Back inside!"

The Prince and Serafine tried to answer but there was no sound. I had no idea where the Silence spell was coming from or how large the zone would be. I paced back and forth furiously breathing quick short breaths. What I had heard in the darkness before the spell was the footfalls of hundreds.

I looked toward Serafine and saw something I had never seen in her. Fear. When she realized who they were after it didn't take long to figure out why. Her power, with no soul to give her the morals not to use it, would result in perhaps the strongest necromancer that had ever existed.

I stopped and took a long breath. My hooded cape dropped to the floor as I unhooked it. Drawing my blades, I sank to kneel before the door. I looked toward her again, not seeing a sorceress or a necromancer that she could become. I saw my partner and friend.

"It will all be okay," I said.

"How can you speak?" she mouthed the words.

"I am a Sword of the Fallanasi, Chosen of the Three…"

CHAPTER TWENTY-THREE

I unclasped the leather armor chest piece and let it fall to the floor.

"My body is my weapon…"

I raised my blades to my lips. "My blades, an extension of my body…"

The familiar words filled the silence around us. I placed the swords on the ground in front of me and touched my lips. A small sigil under my lips glowed yellow."

"I am the voice of Pyra, she who cannot be silenced. It is with her voice I greet thee."

I touched a sigil on my chest that blazed with an ethereal blue glow.

"It is with the heart of Klyn, he who cannot be restrained, I stand before thee."

I stood with red sigils glowing on my forearms. My voice boomed through the night with an inhuman force.

"I am the hand of Tyr, the relentless. With his hand, I slay thee!"

I looked back at the Prince with eyes glowing a brilliant white.

"Nothing reaches her." My voice was a combination of many voices.

The Prince nodded with wide eyes and drew a pair of short blades.

I turned back toward the door and time seemed to freeze.

"My sweet Asmodaeos Kortalis." Her voice washed over me with a terrifying bliss. "We would never ask you to do this again. My Chosen, my favored."

"You didn't, Lady. I chose this."

"But the price…"

"Will be paid willingly."

"The first time we asked and you paid the price to save a hundred thousand of our people. You would pay the price, the ultimate price, now for one? You may claim it is to prevent another necromancer but we see you, Asmodaeos. One swift strike of your blade can remove her. One strike with the hand of Tyr and she would be unable to be brought back. You have seen the price when an older sword invokes us. Half of our Chosen never survived Tyranis."

"I know the price, my Lady. Would I pay it

for thousands? Yes. Would I pay it for one? For her? Yes."

She stood in front of me, beauty incarnate. Pyra stooped down and placed a kiss upon my lips.

She straightened back up. "You are incomparable, my Chosen. Although it saddens me greatly, we will give you what you ask."

She motioned toward the door. "Shall we?"

I pushed the door open and stepped out into the night with a silent horde of the dead closing in.

There is an ecstasy that comes with channeling the power of a god. A feeling like no other. The price is always steep but the gift is immense. When the Priestess of Shalira had healed me she paid the price for it by taking every wound upon herself. I hadn't been coherent for that part, but afterward, I saw her face when she was in the embrace of her goddess.

The pact with the Three was a direct link with my gods. My price would be to pay after. The last time had left me enfeebled and near death's door. This time would undoubtedly send me through that door.

But in this very moment, I was filled with the glory of three gods. My body was covered in blue-etched armor that shrugged off blows that would topple a horse. My blades made sweeping arcs that launched red flame across the dead army. And my voice shattered flesh, bone, and even stone in places.

I swept through the army of the dead leaving nothing in my wake. Then I spotted the form on the city wall moving his hands in patterns meant to raise the dead behind me.

I leapt over five hundred feet to land at the foot of the wall and then jumped straight up to land beside him.

"Judgement day, necromancer."

"If you kill me, I will come back more powerful than ever!"

Pyra took control of my body. "Necromancy is of mortals. Know ye, foul one. You do not face mortal magic. You face a Goddess. You have already cost us more than you will ever know and you will *not* be coming back. Now hear the voice of the divine."

I felt the power from every part of my being as Pyra spoke through me. Her voice took form as a channel of raw power and a scream that was undoubtedly heard through all of Rhyme. The necromancer was completely obliterated there in front of me and the city wall below me ruptured and collapsed.

My feet never left the stone I stood upon

as it plummeted to the ground. There was no shock of landing and I walked out of the dust cloud to see all of the remaining dead had collapsed with the death of the necromancer.

Once again, Pyra stood before me in a moment between seconds.

She stooped down to kiss me again. "Goodbye my Chosen. The pact is irrevocable. If I could change it, I would for you. You were always my favorite."

I touched her cheek. "Goodbye my Lady. I will miss you."

To my astonishment, a tear rolled down her cheek to drop at our feet. The ground shook as it impacted. And she was gone.

I fell to my knees as the Three left me, then toppled to the ground. My body began to twist and agony filled me.

My skin shrank and aged, muscle began to waste away. I was already well past where my first use of the gods had taken me and my vision began to fade.

Through the burning pain I felt a coolness as someone lifted me from the ground. My eyes opened to see a beautiful face looking down at me as she held me like a small child.

"Asmodeaos Kortalis."

Her voice was all around me, even inside me. I felt every syllable in my bones.

"You are known to me. My children chose well."

"Wh…what?"

"I am Sylvyne, Mother of the Gods."

Strength was beginning to fill me again.

"I cannot reverse the pact between mortal and divine any more than my daughter can. But I can give you my strength for just a moment."

One hand rested on my chest.

"The price?" I gasped.

"You have already paid the price. You gave everything to save a child of Sylvyne. That is price enough for a single moment's strength. Remember, Asmodaeos Kortalis, You are Chosen of many more than the Three. You are Chosen of the Light."

The last few words seemed to echo throughout my being as she laid me gently on the ground. As she stepped back and faded away, the pain returned but it wasn't any worse than the first time in Tyranis and stopped after a time.

"Apparently I will live," I said in an old man's voice.

"Kort!"

Serafine knelt beside me. "What did you do?"

"I am a Sword… Fallanasi…" My world faded to black.

CHAPTER TWENTY-FOUR

I awoke in a room filled with white, recognizing the Noskomeon immediately. We had been in a similar room with Marcus Pel's last victim in the not too distant past.

Hearing a light snore, I turned my head which awoke a pain in my neck. Serafine slept curled up in a chair in the corner.

Had it been a dream? Had I truly seen Sylvyne? I had to have seen her or I wouldn't be here at all. I should have been well past death's door.

My eyes landed on an ornate box sitting on the table and I reached for it with a shaky hand.

"I will get it." Serafine moved from her chair to the table. "It was found under you when we picked you up. The Prince wouldn't let anyone touch it and brought it to you."

She handed me the box. Inside was a

glimmering yellow jewel. It almost glowed with a familiar light.

"The Prince said it was of the divine and thus, a gift for you. Everyone knows divinities will find their way to where they belong and he believed it belonged with you."

Pyra's tear.

"Thank him for me," I said in a raspy old voice.

"What happened out there? I saw… I'm not even sure what I saw."

A Medic poked her head inside of the room, "You have a visitor. A Priestess of Shalira. Will you see her?"

"Yes," I rasped.

She entered. I remembered Diana from the time she had healed me.

"What can I do for you, Lady?" I asked as Serafine stepped back closer to her chair.

"I have a message from my Matron." She touched my hand. "She is a Goddess of healing, not warriors, but she wishes you to hear that you are *known*, Chosen of the Light."

Her hand glowed for a moment and when she took it away there was a small sigil on the palm of my hand.

She nodded toward Serafine and left.

"Well that was weird," she said.

"You have no idea," I muttered as my eyes got heavy.

"Sleep," she said. "I will go let your girl know what is going on."

"Thank you," I muttered as I drifted off to sleep with visions of towering beautiful women looking down upon me.

I am a Sword of the Fall—

I looked at the towering forms of the Three. Behind them stood Sylvyne and Shalira alongside many more I didn't know.

I am a Sword, Chosen of the Light.

Pyra nodded her approval, as did Klyn and Tyr.

Then I was alone in my slumber.

I awoke this time to find Sergeant Donovan sitting in the chair.

"Sir," I said.

"You, my friend, have turned Rhyme on its ear."

"Just doing my job, boss. I'm sorry about Simms."

"I never suspected he was a necromancer's thrall."

"There's no telling when it happened," I said.

"Serafine tells me the thralls all died with the necromancer, which brings me to my next kernel of shitty news. Rhyme has been plagued with mysterious deaths throughout the city. The strange part is that they all died at the same time two nights ago."

"Thralls."

"Yes. Including the Chancellor, Councilman Pel, and two Marine Captains."

"Damn," I muttered.

"Better than having necromancer thralls in charge of the city, which was where this was going. Besides, Pel was making a lot of noise about a certain Marine who had executed his son. I say good riddance on that one. But the city is reeling with all of the random deaths from all walks of life."

"How many?"

"Well over eight thousand at the latest count. One thousand three hundred and forty two at the cemetery."

"Damn."

"That's what I said." He stood up. "I'll leave you be for a while but the Marine Commander is going to want to talk to you when you're up to it."

He motioned toward me. "This is not something we are familiar with."

"It will heal… over time."

He let out a long breath. "Good. Not ready to lose one of my best investigators."

"She's the investigator. I just stab them til they aren't a problem anymore."

Donovan chuckled. "Get some rest."

CHAPTER TWENTY-FIVE

I sat on the bench in front of Boggan's Tavern, a small pack at my feet. I could see Serafine approaching as the crowds seemed to split around her.

She stepped onto the porch and sat beside me on the bench. "I'm sorry about Alicia."

"Boggan said she was acting strange for the last few days before it happened."

"She was your Alicia when you last saw her," she said. "Try to keep that memory. Sometimes it helps."

After the events with Marcus Pel, I expected she knew what she was talking about.

"The Commander is waiting," she said and helped me to my feet.

I could see worry in her eyes.

"It will heal over time."

"How much time?"

"Last time, close to a year."

She glanced down at the palm of my hand. "Shalira? You thinking of converting?"

I chuckled, touching lips, chest, and arm in order.

"And another sigil on your chest of Sylvyne. You still haven't told me what happened out there."

"Using divine power always has a price."

"I gathered that. But the new sigils…"

"There's no use worrying about it."

"But it's like a new one pops up every day."

I chuckled.

"You're not going to tell me, are you?"

I grinned.

"That's mean. Just mean."

I pulled a sleeve up over my shoulder. "Have you seen the newest?"

"Another one?" She peered at the sigil. "Marivale, God of the Harvest?"

I shrugged.

She let out an exasperated sigh. "Now I have to look it up."

I chuckled.

We entered Marine Command and I looked at the stairwell leading to the Commander's office

"Excuse me, Mister Kort."

I turned to find a young Marine.

He pointed to our left. "The Commander will meet you in there."

"Thank the gods," I said. "I'm not sure I could have gotten up those stairs."

He led us through a door to a meeting room.

We both saluted the Marine Commander who was an older fellow who still had the muscular build of a warrior albeit aged past a warrior's prime.

"Welcome."

"Commander." I nodded.

"Let's get right to it then," he said. "Despite the lamentations of a certain Major, I have decided to open a Special Investigators Unit. This unit is only answerable to the Marine Commander. I want you two to lead it."

"I'm not really fit to—"

"Nonsense. I am assured this is a temporary state and you shall do nicely."

A few moments later, stunned, I stood outside of the meeting room with a grinning sorceress.

"You already knew about this?"

"Maybe."

"Asshole."

"So now are you going to tell me about the sigils?"

"Nope."

"Going to design our headquarters with no door. You'll have to use dimension doors every time you—"

"Lacrosias."

"The Hunter." She looked perplexed. "I could have sworn that was Marivale. Now I'll have to double check it."

"If you're not going to believe me anyway, why ask?"

"It's more fun that way."

"Asshole," I muttered.

She chuckled as she helped me down the step to the street. "Come on, old man."

Christopher Woods, writer of fiction, teller of tales, and professional liar was born way too long ago to be talking about it and has spent the majority of his life with a book in hand. He is known for his popular Soulguard series and creating the shared universe in The Fallen World series. He has also written the Legend series in the Four Horsemen Universe as well as several works in the Salvage system universe. With books ranging from fantasy to post-apocalyptic and military science fiction, there should be something for everyone. He lives in Woodbury, TN with his wife Wendy. As a carpenter of forty years, he spends his time between various building projects and writing new books. To contact him, go to www.theprofessionalliar.com and send him a message.

BOOKS BY CHRISTOPHER WOODS

Soulguard series:

Soulguard

Soullord

Bloodlord

Rash'Tor'Ri

Freedom's Prophet

Legend series:

Fistful of Credits (anthology)

Legend

Luck is not a Factor (anthology)

Daskada, the Legend

Koreverone, the Legend (upcoming)

Fallen World series:

This Fallen World

From the Ashes (anthology)

Farmer's Creed

The Island of Doctor Laroue (with Chris Kennedy)

Among the Embers (anthology)

Kade (short story collection)

B.E.N.T series:

Annoyed With Lloyd

Salvage System Universe:

Salvage Conquest (anthology)

Through the Gate (anthology)

Smuggler's Run (with William Joseph Roberts)

It Takes all Kinds (anthology)

Car Warriors series:

Go Hard or Go Home (anthology)

Marathon of Madness

Charity anthologies:

Give Me LibertyCon

Onward LibertyCon

Other Anthologies:

We Dare

We Dare: Semper Paratus

We Dare: Wanted, Dead or Alive

The Dogs of God

It Came From the Trailer Park

It Came From the Trailer Park 2

It Came From the Trailer Park 3

Starflight: Tales From the Starport Lounge

Thirteen Stories of Horror

When Valor Must Hold

Children of the Corner

www.ingramcontent.com/pod-product-compliance
Lightning Source LLC
Chambersburg PA
CBHW040534170726
48295CB00012B/469